WEE PIGGIES OF RADIANT MIGHT

BILL MCCURRY

Copyright © 2019 Bill McCurry

Wee Piggies of Radiant Might

First Edition, March 2019

Infinite Monkeys Publishing

Carrollton, Texas

Bill-McCurry.com

Editing: Shayla Raquel, ShaylaRaquel.com

Cover Design: Monica Haynes, TheThatchery.com

Interior Formatting: Rogena Mitchell-Jones, RogenaMitchell.com

ISBN-13: 978-0-9848062-4-9

To Kathleen:the best dance partner ever.

ONE

(Fingit)

These days, Fingit announced himself when visiting the Father of the Gods, hoping to prevent awkward situations, such as the day he found the old fellow squatting naked in a ditch, giggling and weaving grass into his beard. One could expect eccentricity, especially since existence was so bad just now, but that kind of behavior was disturbing to see in the most powerful of all divine beings.

"Father!" Fingit walked down the tree-blemished hill. Although spring was well along, the trees looked poor. Not diseased, just washed out and puny. He squinted through his spectacles and wondered if he needed stronger ones already. "Father!" Fingit puffed on down the hill with purpose, his modest gut waddling.

The hill led down to a precipice overlooking an immense drab valley bisected by a meandering, muddy river. An ancient stone bench perched at the cliff's edge. It was ancient in a profound way, since it dated back to the beginning of time as the gods understood it. Krak, Father of the Gods, sat leaning forward on the bench he had built, facing the valley.

Fingit frowned at the back of his father's head. *He's ignoring me. Damn him. Typical. He wants me to scrape and kiss his feet, in spite of everything.*

When Fingit reached Krak, he stood behind his father's right shoulder and waited to be acknowledged. Krak did not choose to acknowledge him at that time. During the wait, Fingit examined his father. The old man's hair looked thinner than yesterday, and not just white—almost translucent. His stubbly face did not appear noble and craggy anymore. It looked like crumbled stone in a worn-out net. Brown spots speckled his white sleeve.

Crap... his robe is stained. Is he that far gone?

Five minutes passed, and with supernatural force of will, Fingit managed not to squirm. *He's doing this on purpose! The vindictive old turd!*

At last, Krak drew a deep breath and said, "My son. What do you want? I'm busy."

"Um... busy with what, Father?"

"Contemplating the existence of my foot up your ass."

"Huh. You should be nice to me, Father. Nobody else pays attention to you anymore. The worse things get, the more they forget about you."

"The little thugs." Krak leaned back and patted the bench beside him, and his youngest son stepped around to seat himself with a sigh of non-divine relief.

Krak glanced sideways at his son. "So, what are you here to tell the old fellow today?"

"Things are great. Better than ever. Trutch just sits under that dead tree and whines all day. Effla has been banging demigods three at a time, and Weldt doesn't even care. He just drinks wine and makes up songs about lightning bolts and whales." He paused, but his father just leaned forward and grunted. "Lutigan stabbed

Chira's flying moose through the heart—fourteen times—and then ran naked through the Emerald Grove, pissing on every fourteenth tree."

"Anything else?"

Fingit cleared his throat. "Well... Sakaj committed suicide."

Krak groaned. "How?"

"She stabbed herself through the eye with a thorn from the Tree of Mercy." Fingit said it as fast as he could.

His father lifted his head. "That's not so bad."

Fingit glanced down at the side of the bench and brushed off some nonexistent dirt. *Father's perspective on "bad" has become skewed. Or maybe screwed up to holy hell.*

"She did it just the one time?"

Fingit nodded. Sakaj had once committed suicide every day for a year, and she'd never employed the same method twice. She began with hanging, drowning, decapitation, and all the popular ones. Then she got creative. She crushed herself between rolling boulders. She called Lutigan childish names for fourteen hours straight until he chopped her into fourteen pieces. She threw herself under the Holy Bulls; she tore out her own hair and hanged herself with it; she chewed her hands off and bled to death. Of course, she was reborn each morning. She was a god, after all. But she certainly looked worse and worse every day, and her behavior disturbed everyone else in the Home of the Gods.

After her Year of Self-Annihilation, Sakaj stopped committing suicide and had never spoken to anyone since. She wandered through the withering forests. That was annoying behavior too, but at least one didn't find parts of Sakaj scattered around when going to pick golden apples.

Well, they were tin apples now. As existence had grown sadder and less robust, so had the apples. When the crisis had broken, the golden apples became silver in a blink, sweet but no longer a near-sexual experience. Soon, the sliver tarnished, producing firm but unexciting fruit. The bronze apples came next and weren't so bad, mealy but wholesome. Later, the bitter iron apples forced the gods to chew a lot to get them down, and the current tin apples left a film on the teeth and just tasted nasty. An industry of manic wagering had arisen speculating on the next apple degradation. The current favorite was stone, although a militant minority claimed that copper had been unfairly skipped, which would soon be rectified by the laws of existence.

But that wasn't the point. The point was that Sakaj had resumed murdering herself.

"So, Father, any advice from the divine fount of knowledge?" Fingit failed to keep the sarcasm out of his voice.

"Screw 'em!" Krak sounded almost like his old, mighty self. "Let's you and me head down into that valley with a couple of cute broads and a barrel of wine, and leave these fools up here to obliterate themselves."

Fingit stared at his father. "Do you mean that?"

Krak giggled, looked back into the valley, and ignored Fingit.

Fingit leaned back, closed his eyes, and reflected on how impotent the once-omnipotent Krak had become and what that meant for everybody. *I never appreciated what we had. Men were always begging to give us power and gifts and their virgin daughters. Then, BAP! Whatever the hell it was fell between us and man, and damn it to the Void for eternity. No more men, no more power. No more virgins, either.*

"Father, what do you want me to do? I think the crisis is here. We must do something, or soon we'll be too weak and stupid to do anything. Don't you want virgins anymore?"

"Just a little more time," Krak mumbled.

"It's been eight years! Just tell me what to do!"

"I could use a drink and a chubby nymph..."

Fingit rose with a grunt. "Nice chat, Father. If you think of anything that can save us from an eternity of madness, misery, and terror, you might mention it. You know, just in case it comes to you while you're picking your toes. I'll be in my workshop making a poorly designed machine for doing something pointless, and which won't work anyway. If I'm lucky." He hurled an impossibly searing glare over his shoulder and then waddled back uphill.

Fingit began wheezing. Glancing up, he spotted Sakaj clinging high in a wasted pine tree.

Is that her executioner today? Is she going to brush her esophagus with a pine tree? Hah! Who cares?

Sakaj normally remained inscrutable and creepy. Therefore, when she began shrieking and throwing pine cones at Fingit, he stopped and squinted at her. Her actions perplexed him. Otherwise, she looked the same as she did every other day—filthy and crazy as hell.

Fingit glanced back toward Krak to see whether the old man was paying attention to his daughter's more-bizarre-than-usual behavior. Fingit was therefore the first to see a monstrous, green-scaled hand appear from over the precipice and slam into the ground not far from the bench, launching clods of earth high into the air. The hand was enormous enough to seize two chariots at once, and it bore claws as long as Fingit was tall. Monstrous was indeed the proper way to describe this hand, since it belonged to a literal monster.

"Cheg-Cheg," Fingit whispered.

In the next moment, the gargantuan, purple-feathered head of Cheg-Cheg, Dark Annihilator of the Void and Vicinity, rose from below the precipice. Its great, furnace-bright eyes squinted at Krak. Its maw—which could eat four chariots at once—opened and released a roar that promised unremitting destruction. The immense volume smashed Fingit onto his back.

Fingit sat up, blood streaming from his ears and nose, and he saw the beast clambering up onto the precipice. Based on eons of fighting this creature, he knew it would continue clambering until its entire three-hundred-foot-tall self eclipsed the bench, Krak, Sakaj, Fingit, and all the pine trees within sight.

Cheg-Cheg had, from time to time, made war on the gods, at intervals mysterious to even the cleverest among them, or at least to Fingit, who considered himself the cleverest. No one knew why the monster appeared from the Void to assault the gods and all their works, but in each conflict, the gods had prevailed only by employing all of their might and guile.

The Annihilator was now stalking the gods' realm again, but the gods had grown punier than a modest breeze. Krak hadn't summoned the impossibly searing light of the sun in years. Fingit's Hammer That Crushes Souls was propped in the corner of his workshop with dirty laundry hanging on it. All that the gods had remaining was guile.

Fingit employed all of his guile by standing, running away three steps, running back toward the monster five steps, and halting with a slack mouth and twitching eyes. Krak stumbled uphill just as Cheg-Cheg snatched the timeless granite bench and shoved it into his maw. The landmark disappeared with a rumbling clatter of teeth against stone.

Krak slipped to his knees, and Fingit sprinted to help his father. Just one stride away from the old man, Fingit encountered one of Cheg-Cheg's immense, leathery black feet capable of crushing twenty demigods with one stomp. One of the foot's pearl-white claws smacked Fingit an incomprehensible blow. Fingit's skin hurtled fifty paces away, carrying inside it dozens of smashed bones and a fair number of ruptured organs. He landed on his side, almost blind with pain and unable to move, speak, or breathe.

Before Fingit's eyesight faded, he saw Cheg-Cheg bend down and slice Krak in half as if plucking a daffodil. His blood splattered over a great expanse of sad grass that perhaps hoped to be better nourished on this divine blood. The monster seized both halves of sundered Krak, hurled one across the valley, and chucked the other uphill over the horizon. Fingit wept as he watched his father's majestic head flop around on his airborne torso.

Fingit was losing the ability to feel pain when Cheg-Cheg grabbed his destroyed body. The monster hauled Fingit up high above the bloody, grassy ground. As he dangled Fingit above his fetid maw and prepared to consume him, Fingit closed his eyes.

I hope Dad doesn't act like a jackass about my letting him get cut in two.

TWO

(Fingit)

F ingit strained and distorted his face for several seconds before his left eyelid opened, ripping through a light film of dried blood. His right eye didn't respond at all, so it was probably a lost cause. A shapely leg lay in front of his face. It was clad in purple silk and would have been lovely were it still attached to the goddess lying nearby. Cassarak, the Goddess of Health, wasn't looking her best, either. Besides missing two limbs, her body had been crushed and pummeled so that it resembled a cud chewed by a nervous camel, but less wholesome.

Looking past the dismembered limb, Fingit saw that he was in a familiar forest and twilight rested upon it. The forest looked healthier than the one in which Cheg-Cheg had masticated him to death. It felt peaceful and quite still. Fingit sensed no breeze, and he heard no noises at all. No swishing of tree limbs, no crying of birds—just silence.

Fingit tried to speak, but his crushed jaw was jammed into the grass and his mutilated body lacked the power to turn his head.

Crap! I have to waste a whole day in the Dim Lands.

Someone else spoke. "Stay out of my way next time, you bouncing shit-ball!" Lutigan slurred. It sounded like he was talking through a mouthful of shattered teeth. "But for you, I'd have vanquished the monster!"

"You couldn't vanquish a thimble of beer," a woman's voice wheezed. "Nor a willing nymph, even if she were tied to a post and oiled like a squab." It sounded like Effla, Goddess of Love, and her lungs must have been perforated by at least three ribs.

Lutigan mouthed a protest, and Effla huffed an insult. Several other gods hissed or moaned or gurgled their own opinions. Someone was even slapping a limb against the grass, trying to communicate some vital piece of inane, unhelpful information.

Fingit shut them out. *They're all as crazy as a crocodile humping a couch. If we don't chase away Cheg-Cheg, then every day we're going to get smashed into puddles of flesh and spend all day and night here. And when we're reborn at dawn, Cheg-Cheg will smash us into puddles again. And why's he back so soon, anyway?*

It wasn't as if the gods never received visitors. Beings other than themselves sometimes traveled close to the Gods' Realm. The gods mostly ignored them, although they used a few for specific purposes. For example, Krak invited the Black Drifting Whores of the Universe to a festival every five hundred years to reconsecrate the walls defending the Home of the Gods. The Black Drifting Whores got to feel important, and they brought snacks. The Unnamed Mother of All Existence wandered by the Gods' Realm every few hundred years to provide unwanted advice in exchange for a new wardrobe and some nice jewelry. She and Krak were rumored to enjoy a tryst when she visited, but no one knew for sure. He had been known to agonize over gifts for her, especially shoes.

But the least welcome of all these beings was Cheg-Cheg, Dark Annihilator of the Void and Vicinity. Every so often,

Cheg-Cheg showed up like some dread pig charging the trough, instigating a war that could last for years. Demigods fell like snow, and the gods spent a lot of time in the Dim Lands. The gods referred to these as the Wars of Shattering Woe, but in an odd way, they relieved boredom, which was an immortal being's greatest enemy. After Cheg-Cheg had pulverized or eaten each of the gods several dozen times, obliterated most of the holy buildings, and hauled himself to the peak of Mount Humility for a bit of triumphant roaring, the gods would mount some clever and devastating offensive. They had never killed the monster, but when they hurt it enough, it would flee into the Void. At least, that was how the monster's retreat was described in the songs that gods wrote about their victories. It had always seemed to Fingit that Cheg-Cheg just got bored and wandered off.

But now, without the power they normally fleeced from mankind, the gods were incalculably diminished. Maybe Cheg-Cheg would terrorize them forever. Maybe he'd find that weak, confused gods can be killed for all time. Could they? Who knew?

"Everybody who doesn't want to be tortured for all eternity had better shut up!" croaked the Father of the Gods. Even insane and bisected Krak could slap everyone into silence with his voice. "Did that bastard knock us all off? Sound off when I call you. Harik?"

"Here."

"Fingit?"

Fingit managed to indicate his presence by flopping one foot against the god next to him. From the curses, it sounded like Weldt, the God of Commerce. Krak ran through the list until he reached Sakaj last of all. Sakaj always came last when Krak called his twelve children. She was last on every list. When she protested and asked why, Krak had just shrugged.

This time when Krak called, Sakaj didn't respond.

Krak grunted, "Her vow of shutting the hell up can be annoying. Who's near Sakaj? Slap her."

No one answered.

"She's not here? She wasn't destroyed like the rest of us? Could she have been killed forever? Did anybody see?"

Some mumbles and whines indicated that no one had seen Sakaj.

"Oh, well," Krak said. "Sakaj isn't the most important thing right now."

Everyone waited for Krak to speak. Many stopped breathing. Some were missing lungs or diaphragms, so they hadn't been breathing to start with.

Krak said, "The important thing is that my ass is itching beyond belief. Is anyone close enough to scratch it for me?"

The gods who could speak then spoke all at once. Most of them expressed their ideas about defeating Cheg-Cheg, although Fressa hooted questions at Krak about where exactly his ass itched.

Fingit tried to ignore them all. Without nasty, ridiculous mankind to dupe out of power, this is what the divine rulers of all existence had degenerated into. *Maybe we deserve to be exterminated*, he thought.

When the veil between god and man had fallen eight years ago, it had ripped away contact with mankind like tearing off a scab. After the shock had dissipated, all the gods marched around shouting for the first month while waiting for things to go back to normal. When nothing improved, they sharpened their enchanted weapons, slapped on their golden armor, and practiced raising volcanoes and throwing down deluges. They felt pretty good about that, being mighty and divine and everything. But mankind remained unreachable, and the war-lust faded.

For the next two years, the gods made a lot of plans about what they would do when they returned to the world of man.

They speculated on what might have changed, what mankind had probably screwed up, and how best to fix things. Krak gave unto each of them a domain to command when the world of man was reclaimed.

After those two years had passed, the gods became discouraged and began fighting among themselves. The dismemberments and immolations weren't so bad, but once the gods began wiping out demigods wholesale, Krak showed that he still had the largest balls in the universe by putting an end to it. Then came a year of surreptitious rage and bitching by the other gods about Krak's high-handed ways. Several gods tried to overthrow Krak, and he demonstrated how the impossibly searing light of the sun can halt an insurrection when applied to a god's scrotum. Weldt probably still had nightmares about it.

Divine power ran out, and after another year, the gods gave up. This began the time in which gods sat around becoming sadder, older, fatter, and stupider. Everyone was depressed, and no one could stand anyone else's company. Some of the greatest maudlin poetry of all time was composed during that period. Also, during that time, Sakaj embarked upon her Year of Self-Annihilation.

By the sixth year after the Veil had fallen, most of the morose, flaccid, degenerating gods had slid into insanity and aberrant behavior, punctuated by brief periods of tedious lucidity. Fingit thought maybe he'd been spared the worst of that because he spent a lot of time alone in his workshop and had never paid much attention to anything else anyway. He puttered around with various projects and gadgets that became gradually less complex and interesting as his powers diminished. Krak had become weaker, more confused, and more ineffectual each month.

Now, eight years after the Veil had severed the gods from mankind, Fingit lay elevated in the Dim Lands along with most of his family, and that wasn't as much fun as it sounded.

Being "elevated" was in fact the divine equivalent of being temporarily dead and trapped in the Dim Lands until the next sunrise. After several eons, the gods came to find the Dim Lands tedious beyond expression, even for their godlike imaginations. When a few gods began murmuring that they might prefer real death to all this sitting around, Krak decreed that henceforth no god would be called dead but would instead be described as elevated. "Death" sounded pedestrian anyway, like something a goat or a man would do, and unfit for divine beings. It was of course ridiculous to expect gods to feel differently about the Dim Lands just because Krak used a fancy word, but the tactic nonetheless did change the gods' feelings about the whole situation more than they would admit.

Fingit tried to pick out some speck of logic or purpose in the symphony of bullshit around him. *They're all talking about tactics, but they've lost their minds. We should be talking about logistics, not tactics. We need to get the power flowing again, which means we need to cut through to the world of man. It will be an astounding undertaking. It'll be the most heroic and perilous act of this age.*

I wonder who's stupid enough to let me talk them into it?

THREE

(Fingit)

F ingit sighed as he trudged through the grove that had once been considered the loveliest spot in the Home of the Gods. *The Gossamer Forest looks like a troll's toilet.*

Fingit had become accustomed to the trees being brown, even in spring and summer. But today, the leaves drooped in wilted gray clumps that dripped foul-smelling goo and the trunks put him in mind of a leper's leg. The Whispering Brook had once rippled through the middle of the forest, home to bright fish and clever otters. All that remained was a coarse trench of black, viscous mud populated with nondescript but uniformly repulsive reptiles. Fingit didn't want to think about the Falls of Hope and Loss. They had been his favorite retreat, and he resolved not to even walk down to those falls today.

Fingit adjusted his new spectacles. He hadn't ground them quite right, but they were close enough to do the job. He only hoped the same was true of everything he'd tried lately. Yesterday, the gods had enjoyed a reprieve from Cheg-Cheg's war-making.

They didn't know why, and Cheg-Cheg wasn't known for explaining himself.

Fingit had put that day to the best use he could think of. He had sealed himself in the Forge of Thunder and Woe, where he had fashioned his most magnificent works throughout the ages. Ever since the Veil had fallen, his great smithy had gradually transformed itself into a sad clapboard workshop in the back of his home. He still had a small forge and a nice set of tools though, so he retained the grand name for the sake of nostalgia.

Today, he had set about bringing forth his most important creation ever. He would build a chariot to carry a god across the Void, through the Veil, and back into the world of man. Once the Veil was crossed, then all ills plaguing the gods would be set right. Fingit felt positive about that.

A number of technical problems faced Fingit in designing his chariot, but a philosophical problem loomed over all the others. What was the nature of the matter, the gasses, the streams, and the goo that lay between the Gods' Realm and the world of man? And why was it screwed up?

One would think that at some point, since the beginning of time, the gods would have answered the first question. Krak and his brood had intended to answer it, and they had made it a high priority. Yet other, more critical concerns had distracted them age after age. They had required time to build seventeen-story marble palaces for their pets, to write mediocre love poems for saucy demigoddesses, and to sit with their fellow gods looking down on men to place bets on human activities. For example, a popular wagering game involved betting on which man would be the last to drown in a shipwreck.

Yet the gods had not entirely failed in determining what connected them to the world of man. Various gods had spit forth some theories. Without exception, drinking establishments had served as the places in which theories were conceived, and the theories had always been fathered by alcoholic beverages fatal to any non-divine being.

Weldt, the God of Commerce, proposed the first Theory of Ineffable Conjunction during a pause between bouts of weeping over being mocked in the bedchamber by his wife. He envisioned the connection as a tunnel through which the gods could see and move. He described it as dark and scary, with a forbidding aura that only the brave could pierce. Other gods asked Weldt to explain how two gods could see different things through the tunnel simultaneously. He elaborated, "Climb up my ass, you squint! See how you like living with that moist, rutting harpy!" Then he passed out for four days.

Everyone acknowledged that this theory was weak, but it remained the prevailing, and only, theory for thirty thousand years. Shockingly, Lutigan, the God of War, produced the next theory during a drinking contest against Cassarak, the Goddess of Health. During the contest, Lutigan belatedly realized he was going to lose because no being in existence could consume more food or drink than Cassarak. Lutigan leaped atop the table, scattering bottles, pitchers, and glasses. Then he announced the second Theory of Ineffable Conjunction, which held that the realms of god and man are connected by a window. He proclaimed that he needed to run and "write that down," upon which he fled the tavern and avoided losing the contest. The next day, several gods asked him about his theory, and he had obviously given it some thought. He said that more than one god could see different things through the window because it was "real wide." When asked how gods could pass through it to the world of man, he said, "It's a window. Open it, you moron!"

While thirty thousand years had passed between creation of the first and second theories, the third theory followed the second more quickly. In fact, Gorlana, the Goddess of Mercy, announced the third Theory of Ineffable Conjunction nine hours after

Lutigan announced the second theory. Gorlana, Effla, Trutch, and Sakaj were enjoying brunch at the Sun Soul Pavilion the morning after Lutigan's announcement, and Gorlana revealed that the matter connecting the realms was like an egg. After a discreet silence and some sips of morning-time alcoholic beverages, Trutch, the Goddess of Life, asked Gorlana to explain how this was so. Gorlana said, "Oh, I don't know. But it's such a nice image, I think it must be true."

Gorlana's announcement heralded a one-hundred-fifty-thousand-year hiatus for new Theories of Ineffable Conjunction. During that time, the gods preferred not to think about the topic at all, but if compelled to do so, they tended to side with Lutigan.

After those one hundred fifty thousand years had passed, Harik, the God of Death, hit upon the fourth theory. At Krak's annual birthday celebration, his children gave him a mated pair of whales of an extinct species. The gift-wrap ribbon was rather long, as one might expect. As Harik helped his father unwrap the gift, he became mesmerized by the ribbon and wandered off to a corner of the whale-accommodating tavern to consider it. Later, the entire population of the Gods' Realm, including gods, demigods, imps, and whales, sang felicitations to the Father of the Gods. During the song, Harik jumped atop the female whale and began shouting about the fourth Theory of Ineffable Conjunction. Five seconds later, Harik's left arm was vaporized by the impossibly searing light of the sun, and he henceforth became more circumspect about his theory.

Harik held that an immense ribbon connects the realms. While the ribbon had substance, it was woven loosely enough to enable gods to see through it and pass through it. Some of the gods found this theory interesting, and some felt it to be asinine. It never gained much popularity since all the gods feared that Krak disliked it, and they preferred to avoid having their parts vaporized.

In conceiving his chariot, Fingit rejected the ridiculous egg theory immediately. He tossed out the tunnel theory because it couldn't explain multiple perspectives, and because Weldt was an oaf. Of the remaining two theories, Fingit held no strong opinions about which was correct—or which was the least incorrect, as the case may be. He finally chose the window theory. He didn't feel any better about its accuracy, but he could easily make calculations about something straight and rigid, like glass. Calculating vectors and power ratios for something like a ribbon would be a pain in the butt, and he was already getting a headache.

Once Fingit settled on the window theory, he hypothesized about why no one could see through the window anymore. Perhaps the curtains had been drawn. Perhaps someone had let a shrub grow in front of the window. Could the window have been painted over by an inattentive decorator? Maybe someone had just parked their fat ass in front of the window for eight years. Fingit realized that seemed unlikely, but on an inter-dimensional scale, who could say?

Of course, all these impediments were metaphorical, just as the window was a metaphor for conceiving how the connection between the realms worked. Fingit wasn't so far gone that he misunderstood that. He considered the window metaphor as he conceptualized his chariot and its capabilities.

Fingit then opened his tome of schematics and design notes and studied everything he had written over the ages about chariots. The first thing he noted was to avoid putting anything inside the chariot that should not be touched. In fact, he had underlined that point with red ink.

Quite a few millennia earlier, Fingit had created a marvelous battle engine, the Flying Chariot of Recalcitrant Obliteration. He made a gift of it to Lutigan, who right away went out to create a pretext for attacking somebody unimportant. During the fight, the chariot crashed onto the battlefield on its side and spun for more than two hours, causing Lutigan to vomit up some things that defied identification. When Lutigan complained, Fingit explained that Lutigan must have touched something that should not have been touched. Lutigan observed how clever Fingit had been to place something inside the chariot that shouldn't be touched. Then Lutigan stabbed Fingit fourteen times from his neck down to his groin.

Throughout the day, Fingit amassed information and created a novel schematic for this new chariot, which he decided to call the Chariot of Crushing Divinity. He knew that was an insipid name, but he couldn't think of anything better.

Then Fingit stoked his forge and gathered his materials. Stoking the forge was a huge aggravation. In earlier times, he'd retained several imps to do the scut work around the forge. But when things went to hell, he could no longer feed and house the imps. They turned feral and returned to the forests in the valley.

So, Fingit stoked the forge, fashioned the metal, joined it with cunning, infused it with power he had husbanded for such a task, attended the details of the chariot's appearance, and handled the entire job himself. The day's work produced a brass chariot that gleamed in the divine, though dimmed, sunlight of the Gods' Realm. Fingit smiled upon his work and felt more pride in it than in anything he'd created since the Veil had fallen. He could hardly wait for it to be launched and guided back to the world of man. He just needed to find someone dim enough to ride in it.

After an hour of trudging through the Gossamer Forest, Fingit gave up on finding any stupid gods there. It seemed deserted. He thought he might try his luck down the mountain at the Sun Soul Pavilion, since Weldt and Harik were known to spend evenings there drinking and debauching. Well, their debauching had diminished. Cute demigoddesses once would have toppled onto their backs for these gods unprompted, but now they found Weldt and Harik rather repulsive. The gods sagged unpleasantly, their ears sprouted bountiful harvests of hair, and they were boring in the way only a self-absorbed immortal entity can be. Therefore, the debauching had decreased to almost nothing, and the drinking had increased in proportion.

However, as Fingit walked down the mountain, he spied two figures approaching him. From this distance, one appeared to be throwing a compact net at a small animal, and the net snared the creature without fuss. The accompanying figure ran to the animal, un-snared it, and handed the net back to the first figure.

Fingit hurried to meet these two. When closer, he could tell that the second figure was Gorlana, Goddess of Mercy. Her waves of red hair lacked the luster they had once possessed, and her gown of cream and sapphire didn't swirl with majesty as it had in the old days. Fingit became excited, however, because she was definitely dim. He recognized the other figure by his blood-red armor, tiger-skull helm, and face like a war ax. This was Lutigan, and that dampened Fingit's excitement quite a lot. It wasn't that Lutigan was smart. Lutigan just didn't like Fingit very much.

When Fingit had drawn much nearer to these gods, he again saw Lutigan toss his small net with appalling speed. The net snared a rabbit near the base of a tree, and the rabbit kicked, trying to free itself. Gorlana rushed to the tangled rabbit as Fingit walked toward her. With immense tenderness, she untangled the crea-ture, and then she shot her left hand forth with a black dagger and killed it with a thrust. Almost as rapidly, she reached into her gown and produced six small black spikes. She staked the rabbit to the ground, one spike through each paw and one through each ear.

The Goddess of Mercy rose with less-than-godlike grace and noticed Fingit staring at her in repulsed perplexity. She smiled a sweet smile from her heart-shaped face and said, "Ants have to eat too." She carried the net back to Lutigan with a giggle. He responded with a grimace and an aggressive lowering of his mighty red eyebrows.

"Fingit, what brings you out of your shed? Tired of smelling your own farts?" Lutigan said by way of greeting. Fingit felt hopeful, since this was far more polite than Lutigan had offered in years.

Fingit paused to consider the best way to approach Gorlana and Lutigan. How could he introduce them to the idea of the chariot to produce the highest probability of them agreeing to ride the damned thing? Deep within himself, Fingit feared that the chariot would blow up and vaporize its occupants, so he needed to make this sound really good.

However, Fingit could not think of a lie sufficiently convincing to entice even a moronic god to his destruction. Words and lies didn't happen to be Fingit's strength. He fell back on the same weapon he used when the gods went into battle. He used a gigantic hammerblow between his opponent's eyes—metaphorically, in this case. "I built a chariot to fly to the world of man through the Veil. If we don't get across, all of us will be elevated by Cheg-Cheg or go insane or both. One of you needs to fly it."

Gorlana giggled. "Fingit, you're cute. If you ever speak to me again, about anything at all, I'll stake you out like this rabbit. It'll take more spikes. I'll use nine of them just for your penis." Then she kissed Fingit on the forehead, kissed Lutigan on the ear, and smacked Lutigan a cracking blow on his left buttock. She skipped away, blowing kisses to each staked-out woodland creature as she passed it.

Lutigan watched her. "That was odd."

"It sure was." Fingit nodded.

"She started skipping on her left foot. Normally, she starts on her right. And she's skipping either five steps or six steps between trees, never seven, which would make much more sense. I wonder what this means?"

Fingit closed his eyes and counted imaginary dead Lutigans. "So, about the chariot. Will you ride it?"

Lutigan roared, "Ride it? I already rode it. It crashed onto the battlefield and almost elevated me!"

"No, not that chariot. And I'm sorry about that, as I've said every time we've spoken for the past twenty thousand years. I mean the new chariot that will gloriously save us all."

Lutigan lifted his chin at that, and Fingit saw the God of War's nostrils flare. At the same time, he spotted a figure a hundred paces off behind Lutigan. The intruder was running through the trees toward them.

The Void suck it! I almost have this idiot hooked. Who is that?

Lutigan ended his moment of thought. "No. *You* fly in your stupid chariot. I want to see you vomit up an organ for a change."

Fingit executed a rapid search for a good lie. "I can't fly it. I have to stay here to guide the chariot back to the Home of the Gods. It won't help us otherwise." Looking beyond Lutigan, he saw that the approaching figure was Sakaj. Her Gown of Shimmering Thought now hung stained and shredded on her wasted form. Her hair, once black as a cruel thought and as soft as a lover's breath, now flew tangled in every direction. Fingit saw two beetles crawling in it. Every feature of her once-radiant face was now thrown into such extreme relief that it appeared scratched out in chalk by an angry child.

Fingit ignored Sakaj. "Lutigan, whoever rides the chariot will secure glory everlasting. He'll be the greatest hero in history!" He whispered, "Maybe greater than Krak!"

Lutigan paused with a distant look in his eyes. He opened his mouth to respond, but at that moment, a piercing cry sounded from behind him and both gods looked. Several paces away, Sakaj sat on the withered grass with her sandals off. She had just torn the little toe off her right foot and was in the process of tearing off the toe next to it.

Neither god considered for a moment trying to stop Sakaj. During her Year of Self-Annihilation, some gods had tried to prevent her from harming herself, but she had managed to elevate herself every day no matter what anyone did. They at last stopped trying and learned to accept a shattered, dismembered, or dying Sakaj as part of the landscape.

This current self-mutilation annoyed Fingit, because he couldn't continue hoodwinking Lutigan until Sakaj's howls and shrieks abated. He and the God of War watched Sakaj tear off the second smallest toe on her right foot. Then she went to work on her left foot, tearing off the two smallest toes there as well. She began working on her hands next.

This is unbelievable. Oh, what am I saying? Of course it's believable. She once drank molten lead. This is definitely believable.

Sakaj had torn off the two smallest fingers from her right hand, and as Fingit watched, she used the thumb and two remaining fingers on her gory right hand to rip off the two smallest fingers on her left. She then rose to her feet, grunting and staggering, and glared at Lutigan with incandescent hatred.

"Dumber than dog shit," Lutigan mumbled as Sakaj staggered toward him. Fingit didn't believe she could do more than stagger, but she proved him wrong. She launched herself at Lutigan's crotch, seized his testicles in her claw of a right hand, pulled, and twisted with all her godlike might.

Fingit felt sure that the feral imps in the distant valley heard Lutigan's curse with perfect clarity. Lutigan jumped back, gasping. However, he was the God of War for some excellent reasons. One was that a little unimaginable agony didn't stop him or even make him hesitate. He drew forth one of his fourteen swords that were all fourteen palms long. Inspiration appeared on his face, and striking with the superlative precision of the God of War, he sliced off Sakaj's right thumb. He followed that with the rest of the fingers on her right hand, taking one off with each stroke. He took the three left fingers with lightning cuts, and then he pushed the goddess to the ground so he could deliver three toe-severing strikes to her right foot. As Lutigan began on the left foot, Fingit heard the God of War counting under his breath. "Ten... eleven... twelve..." He counted with each swing of his sword until all twelve of Sakaj's remaining digits dotted the wan grass. Lutigan stood over the squirming Goddess of the Unknowable, chortled, and severed her head as he yelled, "Thirteen..."

Lutigan appeared confused for a moment, and then he looked at Fingit.

"Son of a bitch!" Fingit screamed as joy bloomed on Lutigan's face.

The God of War flourished and bellowed, "Fourteen!" in the same instant his sword swept Fingit's head from his shoulders.

FOUR

(Fingit)

S ince the beginning of his existence, whenever Fingit had been decapitated, crushed, or ripped into bits, he had always returned to consciousness in the Dim Lands. There he'd waited until the sun rose in the Home of the Gods, at which time he'd been restored to his normal, unelevated state.

Certain philosophical questions had arisen from this arrangement. If Fingit returned to consciousness in the Dim Lands, didn't that mean he'd been unconscious at some point? If so, how long had he been unconscious? Since he had been elevated in one place and awoken in a different one, how could he know where this unconsciousness had taken place? And since he was a god, how did he know that existence continued when he wasn't aware of it? Even worse, how could he know that he continued to exist during those times when the universe escaped his notice?

Fingit had thought a lot about these self-contradictory questions. There wasn't much else to do in the Dim Lands while you're waiting to be reborn, especially if you're lying there ripped into bits. He hadn't yet answered the questions to his satisfaction, but while pondering, he had spent many days staring at the Dim Lands themselves. He knew them well.

After being thoroughly elevated by Lutigan, Fingit opened his eyes on a land that was not dim at all. The black sky held a vast, prismatic web of stars. Velvety black grass, edged with reflected starlight, brushed against Fingit's skin. The dense, motionless shadows were probably trees, but they could easily be monsters, worshippers, or statues of naked girls. The air shushed as some invisible creature glided overhead, and a breeze whiffed against Fingit's forehead.

These were not the Dim Lands.

"Are you awake yet?" Sakaj's voice came from beside him.

Since he hadn't heard Sakaj speak in years, Fingit turned to look at her. Actually, he experienced a complete failure to turn to look at her. He couldn't turn his head at all.

Ah, yes, I was decapitated by that grunting turnip, Lutigan. I'm trapped in the Void knows where, and I'm just a head! Who the hell knows where my body is around here?

Sakaj said, "I'm sorry about arranging for Lutigan to chop off your head, but I had limited options for getting you here."

"Where is here?" Fingit asked, his voice breaking.

"I call it the Dark Lands. You know, we live in the Bright Lands, we are elevated in the Dim Lands, and we... do something else in the Dark Lands. I don't think it has a real name though, so you can call it what you want. Afterworld, Other Realm, Unicorn Town, whatever."

"How did you find it? How did you get me here? How do we get out?"

Sakaj chuckled. "I found it through an enormous amount of agonizing trial and error. I was able to bring you here because of my deep knowledge of the mysteries, and because we elevated at almost the same time and place. Getting out of here will be, well, immensely complicated, to be honest. By the way, I do wish I could have found a different elevation for us. Being a disembodied head is such a handicap. I prefer to commit suicide by snorting sulfuric acid or by swallowing my tongue or something similar. That way, once I get here, I can still walk around and do things."

"All right then, why don't you just drown yourself every day and always have a functional corpse or body or whatever?"

"I have to elevate myself in a different fashion every time." She sounded as if she were explaining how doors work to a child.

"Holy rolling toads, why?"

"Because on the other side, I'm rat-chewing crazy! Do you think that someone sane figured all this out?"

It almost makes a horrifying kind of sense. Or maybe this makes no sense at all. Maybe Sakaj has sucked me into her fishbowl of insanity. Fingit forced his jaw to stop trembling. "Of course, Sakaj, that makes perfect sense. Let's make the best of it until you take us home, which I'm sure will be soon. What is there to do around here? You know, if we were capable of doing something."

Sakaj laughed. "There isn't a single thing to do here. But there is something to see. At least today there is. Look up."

Fingit strained to look up as high as he could, considering that he didn't have much of a neck. He whistled at the mass of stars, as thick as the hair on Krak's chest. "Wow, that's pretty. Those are some really neat constellations. A lot like all the constellations I've seen before over thousands and thousands of years."

"They're just a shade different. Look hard."

Fingit rolled his eyes. *At least I can still do that. All right... plain star, boring star, a cluster of boring stars... that are moving awfully fast. Most of them are sort of sitting there, but once in a while, a group moves around. And the colors—*

"Krak and all his whores!" Fingit hissed.

"Indeed."

"Those are men! Those are men, right there!"

"Yes—"

"That rain-down-damnation enormous tree is..." Fingit's brain flopped like a fish on the riverbank.

"Yes, it is." Sakaj laughed again, louder.

"Have you called them? Can they hear you? Have you done a deal yet? Dammit, I wasted a day on a useless chariot." Fingit squinted and stuck out his jaw, trying to get a better look.

"Fingit, hush! I haven't exactly called them. It's complicated. Subtler than forging a hammer with which to bash things."

Fingit swallowed so hard his head almost toppled over. "We have to tell Krak."

"No!" Sakaj bellowed, and then she paused. "Krak will bring everyone else, and they'll ruin everything like mice in a soup pot. This requires subtlety."

"But Krak—"

"Look at these people, dear Fingit. We know one of them."

Fingit stared so hard his eyes watered. "I think I see... no. They just look like people. Meat that walks around."

"Look at the skinny one sitting on that barrel."

Fingit realized the futility of trying to shake his head. "So?"

"That is the Murderer. We own him."

Fingit squinted. The man sat swinging his legs, listening to five nasty-looking fellows scream abuse at him while their mule watched. The Murderer looked like a rag-picker, not a sorcerer. "Well, great! Call him, trick some power out of the boob, and take us home. I'll make you a weapon, and you can ram it into one of Cheg-Cheg's less impervious places."

Sakaj sighed. "Oh, Fingit. Sadly, it's more complicated than that."

"Shit!" Saliva escaped the corner of Fingit's mouth, and he used his tongue to try to wipe it off. "Why is everything so flipping complicated with you?"

"Well, I am the Goddess of the Unknowable. Don't hate me for that." Her voice caught as she said it.

"All right, I'm sorry. What's so complicated?"

"That was graciously done. I accept your apology. The Murderer owes Harik an undisclosed number of killings. Only Harik knows how many, and no else may deal with the man before the killings are completed. I hate to say anything good about Harik, but that was rather clever. The Murderer was one of those protect-your-fellow-man types, and Harik has bargained him into someone who would hike out of his way to stab cripples in the face. So, do you want to bring Harik into this?"

Fingit grimaced. "No. I wouldn't trust him to spit if a dead mouse was in his mouth. Are we stuck with this Murderer? Aren't there any other sorcerers around?"

"Ah, that brings me to the Freak, one of my daughters. She is flitting around within one thousand miles or so. I had almost emptied her before the Veil fell. It was such an artistic endeavor to twist and pound her from a mincing girl into an iron bar. And that is the center of all this. The Freak has one more thing to offer me, something huge, but I need leverage. I need your help, darling fellow, and I will reward you for providing it."

"No. No, no. I think you're insane, and I'm going to tell Krak about all of this."

"How will you find him? I can just leave you here if I wish." Sakaj purred like a cheetah. "You will be nothing more than a head for the rest of eternity. By the way, has your nose started itching yet?"

Damn, damn, damn it! It's itching now. "Fine. I'll listen, but I'm not promising anything."

"Of course not. Now, wait just a moment." Sakaj closed her eyes and gritted her teeth. The stars above them smeared, swirled, and whipped into a new pattern. "Please observe that repulsive boy tottering along that wet path. His entire being cries out to become a sorcerer. Even though he and I share little synchrony, a month ago I shooed him like a dim chicken toward the Murderer."

"Why not toward the Freak?"

"He already wanted to find the Murderer. The idiot has traveled every direction except the correct one. Had I not pointed him the right way, I suspect he would have perished before he ever found the man."

"Krak's ass, he's ugly. Like he was cursed by a witch and then hit in the face with a wagon."

"Well put. The boy always fiddles with things. Not that. Clothing, sticks, mud—just about anything. He might like to meet you."

This is the first new human we've found to hoodwink since the Veil fell, and I'm the one who gets him? This is the luckiest thing that's happened to me in... ever.

"Here's my proposition," Sakaj said. "This little boy is too young to give us much power. Not enough irony and pain in his life yet. But you get him started, and then we'll orchestrate an opportunity to drain the Freak of her final reservoir. Then you and I will defeat Cheg-Cheg, rip apart the Veil, and enjoy our rewards as the greatest heroes of all time."

She must think I'm dumber than mud. I'll just say yes and get home. Then Krak will fix all this. "It's a deal. Let's get started tomorrow."

"I'm so happy you agree!" Sakaj giggled. Fingit wasn't sure he'd ever heard Sakaj giggle.

The fool sounds as if we're going to a party together.

Sakaj said, "By the way, if you're thinking about betraying me, remember that I can arrange to bring you here whenever I wish, and I can choose to leave you here. I might also have you elevated by an avalanche or by Cheg-Cheg's thunderous foot. Existing as a severed head would seem like a birthday party compared to eternity as a layer of paste."

FIVE

(Fingit)

F ingit rubbed his neck and gazed at the stars swirling in the hollow black sky above Unicorn Town. It was as if mankind's existence were being swallowed up by the gluttonous universe. Currently, the window onto mankind showed nothing but ferocious rain engulfing a trail through a muddy mountain valley. He didn't know how far the valley extended, but it was monotonous enough to make a sheep drown itself out of boredom.

Now that Fingit met Sakaj every day in this place beyond elevation, he had taken to calling it Unicorn Town. He did it to aggravate her, since she'd had him murdered in a horrible fashion by Lutigan, and since she was threatening to trap him into boredom for all eternity.

Fingit grasped his jaw and adjusted his neck, producing several echoing pops.

Maybe I should find some other way to elevate myself.

Sakaj had sworn to Fingit that elevation was an integral part of the process to reach the Dark Lands. Also, she needed to be near him when it happened. Yet she had been unable to reliably elevate both Fingit and herself at the same time and place every day. It required more ingenuity than either of them had expected to pull it off consistently. It certainly required more than Sakaj could summon while she ranted and ate bark and danced around in the Gardens of Abstruse Reflection wearing nothing but live turtles.

After the third day of failure, and the third day of being slaughtered by Cheg-Cheg, Sakaj gave Fingit the secret of reaching Unicorn Town. She did not, however, explain how to escape back home.

The fully revealed method of reaching Unicorn Town disappointed Fingit rather a lot. The complete process was holding Unicorn Town in mind as he was elevated, and he had expected something a bit more arcane. Regardless, in order to reach Unicorn Town, Fingit now needed to exterminate himself each morning before Cheg-Cheg arrived to slaughter each and every god he could find and send them to the Dim Lands.

Sakaj was toad-licking mad in the Gods' Realm, and her demented mind forced her to elevate herself in a different manner every day. Fingit wasn't insane in the Gods' Realm, however, so he could commit suicide the same way every day if he wanted. Like a true engineer, he devoted a lot of thought to the suicide problem. Which method of execution would elevate him with the least pain and also leave him a highly functional body once elevated? He first tried the classic wrist-slashing technique. It did the job and got him to Unicorn Town, but it also left a horrific mess in the tub. No imp servants remained to dispose of the body and tidy up, so he had to clear away his corpse and scrub everything clean by himself the next day. He resolved not to try that again.

Poison had ranked high on his list of possibilities, and it sounded like a tidy way to go. For his second suicide, Fingit procured a large quantity of Black Aftershock, the most virulent poison in existence. One good thing about godhood is being hard to elevate by natural means. But that can sometimes be a bad thing, since Fingit required two gallons of Black Aftershock to do himself in. The stuff tasted like dung, smelled worse, and made him belch like nobody's business. After one suicide by poison, he tossed that method into the waste bin.

On day three, Fingit went with a straightforward hanging by neck until elevated. He found it unutterably prosaic, but it was simple, quick, painless, quiet, and private. He did suffer a stiff neck in Unicorn Town, and it felt creepy to cut down his own dangling corpse each morning before breakfast, but he figured you can't have everything. He had hanged himself to reach Unicorn Town these past two mornings, and he had experienced a satisfactory elevation both times.

What's keeping Sakaj? She wasn't joking when she said there's not a single thing to do here.

Fingit flopped down to sit on the dark but healthy grass, stuck his legs out straight, and pointed his feet. In another few moments, he had kicked off his sandals and was wiggling his toes. He noticed that one of his divine digits had a hangnail, and he grunted in disgust.

Sakaj faded into existence, lying collapsed across the grass with her eyes closed. Several of her ribs protruded from her torso like legs on a crab, and her breastbone sounded like a harmonica when she breathed. She opened her eyes and looked up. Before Fingit could say anything, she raised her hand. "Don't ask." She rolled to her knees and began clambering upright, snapping a rib with her elbow as she stood.

Fingit shrugged and rose, snagging his sandals on the way up. The unwithered grass felt like little kisses between his toes. "I haven't been able to see anything. I think it's going to take the two of us again to get anywhere with this."

Sakaj scanned the sky and chewed her lip. "Let's focus on your little one. He hasn't found the Murderer yet, and I'm worried he's been eaten by a bear or fallen in love with some farm girl. We'll find him. After all, these are just people. It's not as if they have flying chariots or anything." She winked.

Fingit clamped down on an angry reply. *If I ever again talk to a god who doesn't mention Lutigan's grunt-humping flying chariot, I'll buy him a drink and give him a mirror that shows other gods naked.*

Gritting his teeth, Fingit grasped the hand Sakaj offered and felt grateful that she had a hand for him to grasp. Yesterday, she'd committed suicide by throwing herself into the gates that guarded the Gods' Realm, the Inviolate Gates of Eternal Compassion. They had turned her into something like the consistency of dumplings and had mashed off her arms. Fingit had to clasp Sakaj's pulped foot. It had worked, but it was disgusting and just looked stupid.

Sakaj and Fingit merged toward unity of thought and purpose as they reached out to sense the would-be sorcerer's presence.

"Go left," Sakaj murmured.

"I don't think so."

"Definitely left. Trust me."

Fingit squinted at her. "That's what you said yesterday, and we ended up in a volcano."

Sakaj twisted and poked Fingit with one of her protruding ribs. "There was interference. And the signatures are very similar!"

Fingit hissed. "Let's try fifty-seven degrees to the right then."

Sakaj snapped, "We're not cutting a piece of metal here!" She muttered, "Engineers..."

"Just go right, you spiteful hole!" Fingit yelled.

"Fine!" Sakaj roared, and the sky swirled before settling into a view that shot across the mountains.

"You're going too fast," Fingit muttered.

"Well, slow us down then, you whiner."

"You are so hard to work with," Fingit whined.

"Hah!"

The view zipped along for a minute.

"Wait! Wait! Wait!" Fingit bounced up and down twice. "I feel something!"

Sakaj gritted her teeth and helped Fingit slow the view.

"Just a little right," Fingit whispered. The view edged right and flew across several miles of featureless, rain-soaked mountainsides and grassy valleys.

"Stop!" Fingit and Sakaj yelled at the same time. Within moments, the Unicorn Town sky displayed three people in a small building of stone and timber.

"I see him!" Fingit tightened his grip on Sakaj's hand.

"I see them both. He's sitting right next to the Murderer!"

Fingit dropped her hands. "Oh, great. We should've just looked for the Murderer instead of yelling at each other."

"All right, just relax. Try to call the boy."

Fingit stared at the dripping boy and invited him to chat. Then he begged for his attention. He threatened the boy with curses upon him and everyone he knew if he didn't respond. He pretended to ignore the boy, and then suddenly screamed to shock him into attentiveness.

"Still nothing." Fingit shook his head after a few minutes of effort.

"Maybe you're doing it incorrectly."

Fingit waggled his head at Sakaj as he mimicked her. "No, I'm not doing it incorrectly!" He made an obscene gesture up at the boy's image. "I've tried everything! I can't get him to listen."

"How the mighty have fallen..."

Bitch! Just ignore her. All right, I can't make him listen, but maybe I can listen to him.

Fingit stared back up at the sky and began relaxing one muscle at a time, letting his mind float up into the air. After a while, he heard rain on a wooden roof. He smiled and almost laughed in satisfaction. Then he heard a fireplace crackling. At last, he heard words.

"... skip most of the boring-as-bird-shit religious overtones, and we can go to the heart of the matter."

That's the Murderer talking. He has a sweet voice for such a nasty-looking old scab.

The Murderer went on: "Every time you do magic, it's the result of a juvenile, mean-spirited pissing match with some god. I mean, it's so petty it would embarrass naked children on a dusty street in the nastiest village on civilization's ass."

Well, that's an awfully insulting way of putting things. If he didn't belong to Harik, I'd try to arrange for him to drown on that beer or be trampled by some flabby herbivores.

"Have you ever bartered with your neighbor for a pig or a quilt?" the Murderer asked. "It's exactly like that, except your neighbor is an inconceivably powerful immortal crybaby, and the pig is a three-hundred-foot-tall pillar of fire you need to burn down a city. It's the same thing, fundamentally. Just the details are different."

Fingit heard the boy speak for the first time. "That's crazy."

Yes, it is! Good boy!

"Let me ask you this." The Murderer leaned back. "What does a man have to sacrifice in order to do magic? Or a woman. As a rule, women are better sorcerers than men."

"They have to sacrifice whatever else they might have wanted to do with their life."

"Wrong!"

The boy leaned further forward, palms flat on the table. "A family?"

"Not that, either."

"I... don't..."

"Himself, Desh." Bib tapped himself on the chest. "He trades himself away to the gods, one piece after another."

"What kind of pieces?"

This should be good. I wonder what kind of idiocy and superstition the Murderer believes.

"I'm asking the questions, but I'll humor you in light of your finding out that everything you ever knew was horseshit. A god will make a sorcerer do something, or have something done to him, to get power. Or maybe he'll give up something or accept something he doesn't want. For a little bit of power, the sorcerer could agree to get three bad colds that winter. For more power, he might have to steal money from his brother and throw it in the river. For a lot of power, he might have to take the blame for a murder he didn't do."

Shit... he understands that a little too well. Harik shouldn't have let this man live so long.

"Is this all true? Bib, don't lie to me."

"I'm not lying, son. Now, based on your vast reservoir of sorcery knowledge, what's the greatest danger to a sorcerer?"

"Disintegrating yourself. Well, you did mention it. Also, cooking yourself and blowing yourself up. You know, losing control of the magic."

"Nope. Oh, control can be an annoyance, but the biggest danger is paying too much. Gods will ask a sorcerer to give up memories, forget how they feel about people, do things they thought only a monster would do—until they agreed to do them. A sorcerer has to decide for himself what price is too high, because the gods will take everything they can. In the old days, you'd see sorcerers as crazy as blowflies or wandering in the forest until they froze to death. They traded it all to the gods."

Void suck my toes! The Murderer is like some kind of disease. He's going to ruin that boy!

Fingit tried to think of a way to assassinate the Murderer

without Harik finding out, but he couldn't come up with one. Of course, he couldn't even make his presence known in the world of man right now, so he didn't have a lot of influence over events.

The Murderer continued: "And if you were an actual sorcerer, you might say, 'Bib, how can I avoid paying too much?' I'd tell you to never make the first offer. Making the first offer is a sure way to end up paying too much. Make the god extend the first offer. Do you understand?"

The boy nodded. "Don't pay too much. How do I know if it's too much? What are things worth? How do I know if it's a good deal?"

"There are no good deals. There are bad deals, and there are deals that are less bad."

"You're just trying to confuse me now."

"No, I'm just telling you things that *are* confusing. Last question. What is the most important thing for a sorcerer to know?"

"I used to think it was knowing your enemy. Now I think it might be knowing what you don't know."

"Hah! You should know that sorcery is less about magic than you might think. Mainly it's about looking tough, being sneaky, and waving your hands around a lot."

Sakaj whacked Fingit on the arm. "Do something, you pokey fool! The boy sits there, ripe as a melon."

Fingit let every thought dribble out of his mind except for the boy's essence. He urged all his supernatural will up toward the human and compelled the little meat-clump to heed Fingit's call. To ready himself for the commands of his god. Fingit overwhelmed the boy with the most profound mysteries of his godly being.

Almost a minute passed while Fingit crushed this callow human's capacity to resist.

The boy glanced down for a fraction of a breath and then

continued staring at the Murderer, mesmerized by whatever that grimy old shit-hook of a sorcerer was saying.

Fingit's breath whooshed out of his body, and he shouted an oath that even impolite gods would find unsettling.

Sakaj turned away. "You impotent, insignificant idiot."

Up through the window in the sky, Fingit saw the boy shifted in his chair, bent over, and seized the table leg so hard it creaked. He uttered an appalling psychic scream that could only be heard by supernatural beings with predatory intentions.

Fingit's breath caught. *That's it! That's an open offer right there! He's bemoaning his pathetic ignorance, the fact that everything he ever knew was horseshit. It's the same as beseeching the gods for knowledge and offering up his innocence in exchange.*

"Yes!" Fingit bellowed, almost tripping and falling onto the grass. He drew a tithe of power out of the tiny pool he had reserved against the day he could once again bargain—separate from his reserve for building things. He yelled, "Done!" and dripped power into the boy, where it would lay ready for use when called.

The boy's illusions shattered and released a wave of power back to Fingit, who received a thousand times more than he'd given the boy. One-thousand-to-one was the accepted rate of exchange between gods and humans. At least, it was accepted by the gods. No one cared what humans understood or accepted.

The boy pulled away and stared at the Murderer. "You're crazy! Why did you agree to that?"

Fingit chortled as he drifted away from this conversation and from the world of man. "I made a deal! I got a trade from the little one, the Nub!"

Sakaj turned her back on Fingit. "Why would you call him the Nub?"

"He grabbed that table so hard I thought he was going to tear off his hand and have nothing but a nub left. But who cares? I made a bargain!"

She crossed her arms. "Goody for you."

"Isn't this what you wanted?"

"I did..." The Goddess of the Unknowable faced Fingit and pouted. "I'm glad you're having fun. It's just that I got eviscerated, and I'm not getting anything in return."

"Just wait. I'll get the Nub hooked, and then you can take the Freak for everything she has."

Sakaj smiled and looked almost like her radiant, eternal self. She squeezed Fingit's hand. "You wouldn't make me wait, would you? That's not very gentlemanly. Share just a bit with me."

Fingit pulled away as if the power was something he held in his arms. "You cow! It's mine!" *Maybe I shouldn't have said that to her face.*

Sakaj took a slow step toward him. "Tosh. You wouldn't possess any power at all without me."

"I have plans for it!" *I don't know what they are yet, but when I figure it out, I'm sure I'll need all this power.*

She took another step and touched his arm. "Just a bit, dear. No more than half."

Fingit opened his mouth, but his indignation was so enormous that words couldn't even squeak past it.

"That is, if you'd like to return home anytime in the next age or two." Sakaj patted his cheek.

Smothering Sakaj with a glare of godlike fury and malice, Fingit withdrew half of the Nub's power and flung it toward her, forcing her to scramble to absorb every drop. She didn't show even the faintest irritation. Instead, she giggled. "Thank you."

With the willpower of an immortal being, Fingit forced himself to nod. *Mock me now, you demented slice of toe filth. Maybe you think it's fun to laugh at Fingit, but I'm still a god. I'll break you.*

SIX

F ingit massaged his temples with a low moan and put his spectacles back on. Krak still had Harik pinned to the ground while Gorlana, the Goddess of Mercy, kicked Harik in the ribs and neck over and over. This had been going on for twenty-seven seconds. Fingit had measured it with an engineer's obsessive precision. He had hoped that Lutigan might intervene in the scuffle, but he just reclined on his gold-inlaid chair, swilled ambrosia, and watched the fight. Fressa, the Goddess of Magic, was crushing the Berries of Immortality into juice, dipping her finger in it, and drawing pornographic images on her arm. Fingit glanced at Sakaj and saw that there was no chance of her interfering, since she squatted under the transparent, crystal table, busy rubbing dirt into her ear.

Gods do not often suffer the maladies of mortals, but Fingit's head felt like elephants were frolicking inside it. Hosting a party of seven gods, six of whom are insane, can inspire a headache even in an immortal being.

The fight might not have been so disturbing had Harik, the

God of Death, not been chortling during the entire brutal assault upon his person. Fingit didn't know what had set off the altercation. The gods had been gathered around the table in Fingit's new adamantine gazebo (five gods around the table and one underneath), and the atmosphere had seemed quite convivial. Then Krak had swept Harik off his chair, with Gorlana right behind to deliver a thorough kicking.

As Fingit wondered what to do about all this, Krak released Harik without a word, stood, and wandered back to his chair, with Gorlana trailing him and chatting with nobody at all. Harik rolled on the ground giggling for about ten seconds before he, too, rose and returned to his chair.

Fingit looked down and stared at the gold-inlaid marble floor as he reflected that the other gods who were not present had sunk even deeper into insanity and couldn't comprehend his invitation to this party. After six uninterrupted days of horror, today Cheg-Cheg had again granted a mysterious respite from dismemberments and slaughter. However, the most deranged of the gods had refused Fingit's offer and had chosen to celebrate in other ways, some of which involved burning holy writings, old clothing, or servants.

"Well, I'm sure that was fun," Fingit said, with a weak smile, looking around at his guests. He kept an eye on Sakaj while he continued. "As I was about to say earlier, the Veil may be lifting."

Huh. She's just dumping handfuls of dirt into her cleavage. That probably means she's too crazy to comprehend what's going on. I wonder what Krak will say about her twitchy little Unicorn Town secret.

"The Veil between us and man is lifting!" Fingit repeated for emphasis.

The announcement didn't generate quite the roar of excitement Fingit had hoped. Lutigan produced a long, fruity belch. Gorlana asked, "Don't you have any ginger for this ambrosia?

Tink-Tink and I never drink ambrosia without ginger." Gorlana tossed her head at an unseen person beside her, whom Fingit assumed was her imaginary friend. Harik busied himself slipping pomegranate seeds to Sakaj under the table, which she wolfed as quickly as he offered them.

Only Krak seemed to grasp any of Fingit's message. "Well done, my son!" he bellowed. "Well done! Now we can all be insane together!"

"No!" Fingit yelled. "The Veil can be pierced now. It's become thin in Unicorn Town—" Fingit stopped himself and closed his eyes a moment before continuing. "It's thin in the Dark Lands. Sakaj and I have been there."

"Who *hasn't* been there?" Lutigan sneered as he poured himself more ambrosia. "Hell, I'll send you there right now if you want." Lutigan fingered the sword at his belt and grinned.

Fingit shook his head and gestured around him. "Not the Dim Lands! Look. Look at my workshop! Last week, it was a repulsive hole. Now I've rebuilt it to its glory! How do you think I did that?"

Fressa massaged the table in a sensual way and sniffed. "It took a lot of sexual favors for a lot of imps, I'm sure, but then imps must be inclined to overlook your shortcomings."

Gorlana chortled. "Now, where is that rotting ginger?"

Harik murmured, "I don't feel that your new workshop represents an aesthetic leap forward from the old one. It was quaint, in a doddering and ineffective fashion. This one is quite horrible." He never looked up from feeding Sakaj. He was now popping orange rinds into her mouth, and she chewed them greedily. Fressa climbed under the table and began drawing a penis on Sakaj's cheek.

Fingit said, "Well, it is better, no matter what you say."

Krak leaned forward. "This isn't a very good party. Everyone is angry. There are no naked girls. And where are the unicorn steaks?"

"Everybody listen!" Fingit screamed, and all the other gods paused to look at him. "The Veil is lifting. We can cross it from the Dark Lands. I just struck a trade. How do you think I got all of this?" Fingit lifted his hands to encompass the magnificent workshop, the adamantine gazebo, the chairs inlaid with gold and wood from extinct trees, two winged horses in a nearby paddock, and three imp servants in gold livery waiting by the house. His guests looked around as if noticing all these things for the first time.

Krak stood, radiating a certain watered-down majesty. In rich tones, he said, "Fingit, my son, if I don't get a unicorn steak, I'm going to piss in the ambrosia."

Lutigan leaped across the table and grabbed Krak by the waist, accidentally kicking Gorlana in the face as he went. Krak began beating Lutigan on the head with his ruby-encrusted golden goblet, while Gorlana clamped on to Lutigan's left calf with her teeth. Harik continued feeding Sakaj as if nothing was happening. He had run out of orange peel, so he fed her diamonds as he plucked them off his goblet. Fressa was licking the immortal-berry-juice penis drawing off Sakaj's face.

Fingit sighed and shook his head. He reached behind him to the gazebo wall and quite deliberately touched a "something that should not be touched" switch.

As Fingit had planned, nine dozen needle-sharp spikes that were cunningly hidden in the ceiling swept through the gazebo in waves. One wave swept west to east, another swept south to north, and the third swept at fifty-seven degrees from north as a special present to Sakaj. Fingit himself was handily slain with Unicorn Town in mind as his destination, but he hadn't relied upon the spikes to do the job for every god present.

Once the spikes cleared, fifty gallons of god-obliterating acid rained from the ceiling of the gazebo. It ate through the gazebo contents with happy efficiency. Any god remaining alive at this point would be suffering a quite appalling death, and incidentally would not possess much of a body in Unicorn Town.

The spikes and the acid would almost certainly obliterate any being inside the gazebo, and quite a lot of the gazebo itself. Yet "almost certainly" was not the same as "certainly." Fingit was an engineer, and he worshiped at the altar of redundancy. His final step to achieve effective certainty of destruction was complex but effective. He had placed beneath the gazebo the most precious of his possessions: a pinhead-size dab of the heart of Cheg-Cheg, Dark Annihilator of the Void and Vicinity. He had been hoarding this smidgen of cataclysmic power since the last war. Per standard procedure, this devastating object had lain bound within a tear from the Unnamed Mother of All Existence. Fingit's pre-positioned apparatus dissolved the tear. At that point, the gazebo and all its contents ceased to exist. Fingit believed not only in redundancy but also in over-engineering. The other things that ceased to exist were the workshop, Fingit's house, two winged horses, three imps, and a good part of the cliff on which Fingit's residence had stood.

If anybody survived that, they could just go fight Cheg-Cheg by themselves.

FINGIT AWOKE in Unicorn Town anticipating some confused and excited newcomers. What he got was Sakaj screaming, "Fingit, you gutless bastard!" followed by a brutal kick to his nonliving balls. Fingit toppled forward onto his face, unable to even squeak. Had his stomach not been pierced by two separate spikes, he thought he might have puked for an hour. "I told you not to bring them here, or they'd screw it all up!" he heard Sakaj yell.

A short time later, as Fingit drew a breath, someone jerked him upright by his arm and gave him a tooth-clattering shake. He looked into the face of his father, Krak. Apart from the ragged hole in his forehead, the Father of the Gods looked better than Fingit had seen him in years. Krak frowned threats of anguish down on his son and said, "Boy, did you just elevate every damned one of us?"

Fingit nodded.

Krak lifted Fingit off the ground with his right hand. He pulled off Fingit's spectacles and crushed them in his left hand. "Why did you do that?" Krak asked through gritted teeth.

Had Unicorn Town not been dimmer than a village idiot, Krak would have seen all the color disappear from Fingit's face. Fingit wondered, perhaps too late, what happens when a god is elevated in Unicorn Town. If Krak became infuriated enough to crush Fingit's neck, Fingit might find out in person what elevation was like there. Rather than speaking, he pointed straight up with his free arm. Krak looked up at the mass of colorful, floating points in the sky. He tensed and then relaxed moment by moment, placing Fingit back on his feet.

"What in the name of the Deep and Noxious Places is that?" Krak mumbled.

Fingit glanced around and saw Sakaj hissing into Harik's face, almost touching noses. Gorlana had wandered a short distance away by herself. Fressa, missing one arm where a spike had ripped it off, was leaning back against a tree and watching everybody. Fingit saw no evidence of Lutigan, which instilled some throat-clenching fear.

Fingit staggered as Krak's elbow hit him in the shoulder. *Damn, Father must have grown a foot here!*

"Fingit... what the... what is this? Explain yourself!" Even in his degenerate condition, Krak scowled in a manner that would have immolated non-divine beings in a trice.

"It's just what I said, Father. These are the Dark Lands, and the world of man is up there. The Veil is thin here. We can get through."

"What are you talking about?" Lutigan yelled from behind Fingit, who spun, but no Lutigan stood there. "Where am I?" Lutigan roared from nowhere. "What did you do to me, you floppy rodent's scrotum? I'll elevate you every day for a thousand years!"

Good thing I used the acid too. Or maybe Lutigan just got obliterated at the end. I hope it was the acid. That would have hurt like molten lava diarrhea.

"Leave her alone, you depraved vulture!" Sakaj screamed at Harik. "The Freak is mine! If you ruined yours for all time, that's just your own fault!"

Harik, one eyeball punched out and dangling on his cheek, said, "You fail to see that the most harmonious and beneficial approach is to share the resources available to us. Bitch!"

Gorlana stalked back over to the group and howled, "Aaaau-uuu! Uuuuuuuuu! Aaaaaaeeaaa!" Her mouth had been disman-tled by a spike, but that didn't prevent her from having her say.

Fressa pointed at Gorlana. "Gorlana apologizes for being such an eternal bitch."

Gorlana kicked Fressa in the shin.

"Everyone who doesn't want to be heaved into the Bottomless Chasm of Nightmares had better shut the hell up right now!" Krak roared with the power of twenty bears, which wasn't bad, but was nowhere close to old Krak, who roared with the power of fifty bears and sometimes a murderous hippo or two. All the gods shut up. Krak pointed at Sakaj and said, "Suicide girl—show me."

If time had any intrinsic meaning in Unicorn Town, and Fingit doubted that it could, an hour passed before Krak nodded and said, "Enough."

Sakaj and Fingit had demonstrated the link in the sky, how to move it, and how they had found people with it. They'd shown everyone the Murderer, the Nub, and the Freak. They talked about trying to find other sorcerers with which to bargain.

Harik begin whining about the Murderer and his open-ended debt, and how Sakaj and Fingit needed to share with him. Krak backhanded Harik and told him to shut up and collect the payments on the debt he was already owed, if he could figure out how.

"All right, here's what we will do," Krak said in his commanding, pre-Veil fashion. "We will come here every day. Fingit, you're the only one who's sort of sane on the other side. It will be your job to elevate us all every day and get us here."

Fingit gaped at his father.

"You're a smart boy—figure it out. As a reward, you get a monopoly on any trades with the Nub."

All of the others stared venom at Fingit when they heard that.

"Sakaj, you work on the Freak. Find something she wants and break her down. Gorlana, Fressa, and Lutigan, you search for other trading opportunities. Harik, capitalize on the Murderer's debt—we could use the influx of power." Krak looked around at everyone except the incorporeal Lutigan. "Does everyone understand?"

This is what I wanted. Right? Old, Insane Krak is gone, and Mighty Krak is in charge again. I guess I forgot that Mighty Krak doesn't like me that much.

Fingit nodded and added his voice to the symphony of affirmations.

Krak sighed and looked around. "All right, I'm bored. How do we get back?"

Everyone stared at Fingit. Fingit stared at Sakaj. Sakaj looked off into the darkness of Unicorn Town and pretended not to hear.

"Someone—and I don't care who—has five seconds to tell me how to get home," Krak said. "I may not be able to fry your nipples off with the impossibly searing light of the sun yet, but I can pound any of you thin enough to write poetry on."

Fingit and Sakaj both began talking at once. Harik sneered at them. Fressa hurled a dirt clod at Gorlana, who threw up her arms and walked away, while Lutigan's insubstantial voice cursed everyone in sight. Krak stood with his arms crossed and seemed to grow taller every second. It was therefore easy to understand why no one did anything useful when Cheg-Cheg's head erupted from the ground beneath them.

The upheaval hurled gods in all directions as the monster climbed out of the prodigious hole it had made in the earth of Unicorn Town. Fingit hit the grass rolling and smacked against a black tree trunk. He felt at least one rib crack. By the time he'd dragged himself upright against the trunk, Cheg-Cheg's entire self stood roaring beneath the prismatic Unicorn Town sky.

"Take us back!" Fingit yelled. "Get us out of here!" He staggered toward Sakaj, who was sitting on her butt and shaking her head one hundred feet away. The monster's foot slammed down in between them, crashing into the ground like a meteor. Fingit tripped and fell backward, landing on the grass amid a hail of dirt clods.

Cheg-Cheg twisted, bent, and swept Fressa up with his clawed hand. She flailed her arms and screamed without words, and part of Fingit noted that she hadn't been this articulate in years. The beast grabbed her right foot with the thumb and forefinger of one hand, and her left foot with the thumb and forefinger of the other, employing the delicate grip one might use with some sort of heirloom. Fressa's scream shot up an octave and a half as Cheg-Cheg tore the goddess's legs apart and, with great tenderness, pulled her in two from the legs to the neck.

Half of Fressa plopped down in an untidy pile right next to Fingit, spattering him with intestines. He rolled away from the viscera, sat up, and saw Sakaj running around the monster's clawed toes toward him. He shouted, "Sakaj! Take us home!"

Fingit didn't remember closing his eyes, but he opened them upon the once-radiant sunrise of the Gods' Realm. He sat up on the grass of the dim and sickly Emerald Grove. Krak, once more frail and palsied, was coughing as he rolled onto his belly. Gorlana lay on her back, chatting with her imaginary friend as they pointed at clouds. Sakaj had wrapped her arms around a nasty tree and was kissing it, perhaps with tongue. He looked away as she wrapped one leg around the thing.

Somewhere behind Fingit, Harik cursed and then giggled. Fingit turned to see Lutigan kick the God of Death in the knee. Harik giggled again and limped away downhill. Lutigan wrestled a gummy branch off the tree Sakaj was humping and chased Harik, roaring.

Fingit stood and looked in every direction. "No Fressa. She didn't come back."

"What?" Krak mumbled.

"I think Fressa's dead. Forever."

"Huh. The little squidge didn't give me a birthday present last year, so who cares?" The Father of the Gods sat up and scratched his crotch.

Murdering us all at the same time every day shouldn't be an impossible task. I should just ask Cheg-Cheg for advice.

SEVEN

(Fingit)

Harik bounded away from where Fingit stood with Krak, running toward some gray rotting bushes while Lutigan pursued him. The God of War whacked Harik a glancing blow with a tree limb and then chased him out of sight.

Fingit tried to push his spectacles higher on his nose and then remembered that Krak had just crushed them in Unicorn Town. *All right, my main task is to gather up my family and elevate them. Well, to hell with Sakaj—she can elevate herself, she's good at it. I'll just take insane Krak along to find nutty-as-hell Harik and Lutigan before Cheg-Cheg shows up again. Easy. Catch them first. Then worry about elevating them.*

Fingit grabbed Krak's arm and hauled him upright. The Father of the Gods plopped back onto the dingy grass, chuckled, and lay there as limp as a dead rooster.

"Come on, Father! We have to catch them now!"

Krak answered Fingit with a long raspberry that left a line of drool on Krak's cheek. In Unicorn Town, he'd been the incomparable ruler of all creation. Here he was a gross, whiny old man again.

Fingit had himself devolved into a flabby specimen too diminished to carry even frail old Krak around. He hauled off to kick his father's backside but then stopped himself. He called over to Gorlana. "Will you watch Father and make sure he doesn't crawl away somewhere?"

Gorlana sat up and looked away from Fingit. "Watch him yourself. We're planning a party."

Fingit closed his eyes for a moment. "I wasn't talking to you. I was talking to your friend. She's the most trustworthy one around here."

Gorlana looked at Fingit and smiled like a young girl in love. "Certainly Tink-Tink will watch him! If Father tries to leave, she will tell me which one of his knees to break."

As Fingit trotted away, he uttered an epithet that compared Gorlana unfavorably to a Void-beast's unmentionable parts. Halfway down the hill, he spotted the prismatic spire propelled above the Marketplace of Reticular Diversion. It stood at the center of the Gods' Realm, and while its stock had near evaporated, it should still have everything Fingit required.

An hour later, Fingit jogged and puffed back into the Emerald Grove, leading a puppy on a leash and carrying a monumental spiked hammer over his shoulder. *This ought to do it, although I owe the blacksmith one of those see-the-gods-naked mirrors.*

Krak lay on his back, snoring, just where Fingit had left him. Gorlana stood guard with the same diligence as her invisible friend, which is to say none at all. Fingit couldn't spot Gorlana anywhere in the grove or in the vale below it. *Well, the Void can suck her away. Father is the important one to keep track of.*

Fingit let the inexpressibly adorable white puppy sniff Krak and begin licking the god's face. Krak woke, said, "Puppy!" and collected the fluffy, melon-size beast into his arms as he sat up. It alternated between licking Krak's chin and gazing at the god with enormous, adoring eyes.

"He's all yours." Fingit shifted the appalling hammer to his other shoulder. "Let's go show him to Harik and Lutigan."

"What are you going to do with that?" Krak eyed the weapon.

"Conversation piece." Within moments, Fingit was striding down through the woods, leading Krak and his new puppy, which Krak had named Dominion. Krak made baby talk, Dominion yipped, and Fingit ground his teeth.

Fingit expected to find Harik in the Hall of Ambiguity, a rather nasty tavern where the God of Death sometimes went to hide from his wife. Indeed, Harik was sitting against the back wall slurping a beverage, the scent of which Fingit found repugnant from ten paces away.

"Harik, my son, meet my new friend and heir, Dominion!" Krak lifted the puppy high in both hands. "He's the only being in existence with the subtlety of understanding required to assume the throne when I abdicate."

Harik glanced over the table at the puppy. "It looks rather like an effeminate rodent to me, not that I mean to give offense. Fingit, what in the name of the Void and our mother's chins do you plan to do with that horrible mallet?" Harik, still seated, squirmed away from the hammer while trying to appear like he wasn't squirming.

"Oh, nothing important. Where's Lutigan?"

"I should presume the ruffian is off stabbing someone. Run off and look for him if you're that interested. Perhaps he will stab you." Harik waved a hand to shoo the puppy. Krak had set Dominion down onto the table, and the creature was lapping from Harik's goblet.

Fingit's neck tingled as Cheg-Cheg's distant roar shook dust from the tavern's rafters. "Sorry, Lutigan. Time to go, everybody." He heaved the hammer above his head one-handed. Krak stumbled back a step, and Harik raised one arm against the blow. Fingit thought about Unicorn Town, snatched the puppy's tail, and twisted it hard.

A tidy package of subtle explosives detonated within the miraculously lifelike mechanical puppy Fingit had constructed using a few drops of his remaining power. None but Fingit would have expected the explosion to produce so little destruction inside the tavern. Also, no one else would have expected it to liquefy a divine being's organs into goo in such an efficient manner.

WHEN THEY REACHED UNICORN TOWN, Fingit's puppy-dog ploy earned Fingit a snort and an approving whack on the shoulder from his father. Then Krak growled and smacked Fingit's other shoulder for failing to bring Lutigan and Gorlana. Fingit rubbed his numb arm and composed himself for a day of lurking above the world of man like an immortal vulture.

Sakaj had already arrived, and as his first item of business, Krak demanded that she share the secret of returning home. After several minutes of argument, equivocation, threats, and tears, she told everyone how to do it. It wasn't that hard. Metaphorically, it was comparable to pulling on your trousers inside out and backward, while remembering there's an invisible third trouser leg you have to tie to your wrist. Fingit admitted that he probably never would have figured that out on his own.

Krak stood tall and scowled. "I must return home. I don't see any other way to test whether you're lying about all this, Sakaj. I'll be a drooling worm on the other side, so I won't be back today. I'm trusting you—all three of you—not to screw around like some damned lower beings. I can trust you, can't I?" Krak clenched his fist, in which he had years ago held the impossibly searing light of the sun. That light had flickered out, but the other gods hadn't forgotten, and they nodded assurances.

That left Fingit alone with Sakaj and Harik. The three of them began sniping and bickering over who got to control the window onto the world of man.

"Gorlana."

Fingit looked around. "What?"

"What?" Harik said. Sakaj just frowned.

"Oh, Gorlana..." came a voice from someone who wasn't in Unicorn Town.

"Mother stab me in the heart! Somebody wants to trade!" Fingit said.

"That's the Murderer!" Harik pushed past Fingit and knocked him down, although the voice wasn't coming from any particular direction. "He's mine! Stay away!"

Fingit stood up, glanced at Sakaj, and shrugged. "Sure."

The Murderer began materializing out of the darkness above them.

Whenever humans came to trade, they saw nothing. It was as if their bodies didn't exist. The gods had created the trading environment that way ages ago. However, gods could see humans perfectly well. It gave the gods a nice little advantage when the bargaining became heated. In Unicorn Town, the window lacked most of the style and refinements the gods had enjoyed in their usual bargaining arena, which had burned down, collapsed, and been swallowed by the earth. However, Unicorn Town did possess all the necessary functions.

The Murderer at last arrived, a thin, ragged, middle-aged man. His neat beard and longish hair showed more gray than red. Weather and strain had lined his face, but he exuded a surprising amount of vitality.

And that's the Nub arriving next to him! Balding, freakishly huge cheeks, clean-shaven, young and fit, but unexceptional. Oh, now I see, he's bleeding to death. His leg's just about torn off. Well, that ought to give me a little leverage in negotiations.

The Murderer was speaking, apparently to the Nub. "There are no good deals. Right?"

The Nub nodded. "Right."

"Hush now." The Murderer didn't hush at all when he said it. "I sense a bunch of assholes approaching."

Harik said in a deep, painfully rich but clipped voice, "My dear Murderer, is that an appropriate greeting for an old acquaintance, absent these many years? One to whom you are obligated in such an overwhelming manner?"

"My apologies, mighty Harik. I amend my observation. I sense a bunch of squabbling, grasping assholes with the morals of back-alley drug addicts approaching. Your Worship."

"You might cause me to forget how profitable our little discourses have been, Murderer. Be thankful I remember the profit and choose to allow your continued existence."

The Murderer smirked. "Pretend I said thank you until you blushed, Harik. Was that you creating hell and confusion with all the fog just now? That was a lot of hard work just to get my attention. Do you like me that much? I like hemorrhoids more than I like you."

Sakaj whispered to Harik and Fingit in the divine whisper that the humans would never be able to hear. "Why do you take such abuse from this sad package of meat? I didn't think my opinion of you could fall any lower, Harik, but I believe it has."

Harik whispered, "What do I care for his opinion? I use the fool as if he were one of Fingit's grimy hammers and no more."

Fingit raised his eyebrows and whispered, "Wait. He said fog. Harik, what fog?"

Harik looked mystified, and then he smiled. "I silently wished confusion upon mankind earlier. My unparalleled intellect and power manifested that wish as fog to inconvenience my property, the Murderer." Harik looked up into the distance as if waiting for someone to carve a statue of him.

Sakaj and Fingit stared at Harik for a few seconds until Sakaj shook her head.

The Nub spoke again, and his voice quivered a little. "Bib, is that the voice of the actual God of Death? Shouldn't we be... humbler or something?"

"He's a mighty god, Desh, and he doesn't care what us insignificant nits think. We can't hurt the fussy little moose-crotch's feelings. Can we, Harik?"

"No." Harik ground his teeth and whispered, "You foul insect."

Fingit whispered, "Right, you don't care. He's just a hammer and no more."

The Murderer looked around and smiled, even though he was incapable of seeing anything. "So where have you boys been all these years? Big hangover? Misplace your thunderbolts?"

Fingit bit his lip. *What do we say? We can't say we've been sitting around getting fat and going crazy.*

Sakaj whispered, "Let's just pretend we didn't hear the question." Fingit and Harik nodded.

After a little more silence, the Murderer shrugged. "That's all right, I don't really give a shit. Just making conversation. Besides, I didn't call for you, Harik. I called Gorlana, so why the hell are you here?"

Fingit whispered, "Harik, can't you get him under control? He's teaching the Nub bad habits."

Harik sighed and whispered, "I invite you to make the attempt yourself if you wish. I have never dealt with any sorcerer more willful and profane than this one." Harik spoke out to the humans. "I own you, Murderer. Nothing happens involving you unless I sanction it. I must approve any exceptions, and until you fulfill my debt—"

The Murderer rolled his eyes, even if they did lack substance. "Oh, shut that festering gash in your face, you long-winded fart!"

The Nub said, "Just to be clear... should you be talking that way to the God of Death? I mean when I'm... I mean on the other side, things are..."

Sakaj whispered, "Harik, you should not forget that all this talk of sanctions and exceptions arises from nothing more than convention. From polite agreements between us, that is. Fingit could trade with the Murderer if he chose, regardless of your talk about sanctions."

Harik whispered, "You leave the Murderer alone! He is mine!"

Fingit whispered, "This sorcerer seems to despise you, Harik. To an embarrassing degree. Almost as much as your wife does, if that's possible."

Harik bounded over and stood nose to nose with Fingit. "No one will trade with the Murderer but me, upon pain of my displeasure," he whispered.

Sakaj whispered, "Then hurry and wring something good from him!"

"Fine!" Harik said it out loud where the sorcerers could hear him. His eyes popped wide open. He had allowed sorcerers to hear something he had meant to say only to other gods. It was an embarrassing lack of discipline that could earn him several thousand years of mockery. He glanced to each side like a little boy caught stealing a pie. Then, with eyes still wide, he said out loud, "We're not fools. I know what you want. No one can help you, Murderer, because you cannot pay. I hold a lien on everything you have."

Sakaj whispered, "Harik, would you wish me to speak aloud to the Murderer and tell him what your wife says to everyone about your deficiencies?"

Harik hung his head and whispered, "Damn it to Krak's rod!"

Fingit and Sakaj were laughing silently into their hands.

The Murderer said, "I'm not here to make an offer. I'm just

here to advise Desh on his first deal. To make sure he doesn't get completely violated in a bad place by you jackals."

Harik paused. "You may not negotiate for the other one. Go away."

"No."

"I command you to leave!" Harik boomed.

As calm if he were talking about pie recipes, the Murderer said, "I command you to screw yourself, your sister, and your pet goat. See how far that command goes."

Harik whispered to Fingit, "I cannot force him to leave unless I terminate negotiations. Is that what you wish?"

"No, keep going!"

Harik said out loud, "Fine. You've always been a difficult case. I'll allow you to remain, if you promise to be respectful and quiet."

"Thank you." The Murderer smiled. "So, will you make Desh an offer? Please, O great Harik, who can topple mountains with one quiver of one hair on your masculine, hirsute backside?"

Harik smiled too. "No. I cannot deal with him."

"Do you mean you're wasting our time with all this prancing around? I was nice to you for no reason at all? Come on, Desh, let's go." The two sorcerers began to fade.

Fingit spoke up. "I can trade with the young fellow. Happy to do so."

The Murderer beamed. "Why, that sounds like Fingit! How have you been, Your Worship? Built any good chariots lately?"

I want to destroy this sorcerer so much. Why was I ever nice to him? Fingit forced himself to laugh. "Murderer, I own the exclusive option on the Nub here. All of his trades must go through me."

The Nub scowled. "What? The Nub?"

"Yes, that's our name for you," Fingit said. "We have to call you something evocative. Who can remember all these sorcerers by their sad little human names?"

"Bib gets the Murderer, and I get the Nub? Why the Nub? Why not the Crafter or the Falcon or something like that? No one's going to respect a sorcerer called the Nub."

"We could just call you the Corpse." Harik purred, something he did when he wanted to sound terrifying. The other gods compared it to the many horrible sounds produced by human digestion.

The Murderer said, "None of this matters a damn if we can't make a bargain. Let's get on with it!"

"Quite so!" Fingit pursed his lips. *All right. Come on, we're waiting, Nub. We only have so much time before the end of existence.*

The Murderer cleared his throat. "Desh, they're waiting for you to tell them what you want."

"Oh!" the Nub yelped. After a long pause, he said, "I want to be healed, and I want my leg back."

Fingit whispered, "Let's get them just as confused as a bat in a barrel. Multisided deals, restrictions on possession, options, and whatever else we can think of."

Harik grinned.

Fingit put on a pitying expression so that the sorcerers would hear it in his voice. "Ah, I'm sorry, but that's kind of a problem. You may trade for power, but it becomes *your* power. How will you then use it? Nub, you can't just wave a stick or some chicken entrails at the stump of your leg and expect it to be healed. You must cede the power to the Murderer so he can heal you. For that, you have to deal with Harik."

"Pig shit on apple pie, are all of you bastards trying to get a cut of this deal?" the Murderer said.

Harik said, "Murderer, I know that I've taken a firm stance in the past on clearing your current debt before any more deals, but I am prepared to waive that restriction, this one time only, to assist you in this dire situation."

"Really?" The Murderer's voice oozed sarcasm.

"Truly! I am prepared to offer you a substantial trade. I will grant power enough to completely heal the Nub. I also offer power beyond that, which you may use to heal, bless, call the forces of nature, or anything else within your talents. This will be a large block of power—five complete squares. Just make an offer."

"Just kiss my ass. If you have an offer to make to Desh, make it."

"I'm asking very little of you, really. In addition to the many murders you have already accomplished for me in such a fine fashion, I would require that within the next week, you murder the one person you care about most. Easily done, as I'm sure you'll agree, since those whom you love tend to annoy you beyond all reason quite quickly. My own wife comes to mind."

The Murderer laughed. "No. Definitely no."

"Ah, that is a shame. But as a bit of incentive, I will reduce your open-ended debt in addition to my current extremely generous offer."

"That doesn't mean a damn thing. You could say the debt's cut by a hundred, but only you know how many I still owe. It might be a thousand, or ten thousand."

Harik smiled. "Or one hundred and one."

The Murderer sneered. "I don't trust you, so forget it."

Sakaj whispered, "Harik, how much are you willing to give? Once the Veil comes down, this open-ended debt may be the best deal any of us has."

"We need the power right now," Harik whispered. "A dependable stream of power means nothing if we all get pulled in half and tossed around the landscape."

Harik said to the humans, "Very well. I'm making a tremendous sacrifice here, but I'm prepared to cancel your open-ended debt completely—paid in full—if you kill the person you care about most within the week. I will also deliver five squares so you can save the Nub."

The Murderer looked down and hunched his shoulders. His jaw tightened and relaxed over and over for what seemed like a long time. "I might..."

Fingit peered at the Murderer and whispered, "Oh... is he about to cry? That's embarrassing. You should kill him when we're done, Harik."

The Nub cleared his throat, twice. "Say no. Nothing's worth that. Let's leave."

The Murderer nodded. "All right. Harik, I say no."

"You should reconsider. You will never get a better offer. You'll never even get this offer again."

"On second thought... no. Drop it. My answer will always be no."

Harik whispered a litany of volcanic curses. Then he took a slow breath, although his fists remained clenched. "A shame. Very well, I don't see what we can do for you." He scowled and motioned for Fingit to take over.

The Murderer and the Nub began drifting back to the world of man.

Fingit said, "Wait! There may be a way for us to help, but it won't be cheap."

"Let me guess," the Murderer said. "Desh trades you something you fancy, then you peel off part for yourself before passing it on to that impotent leech, Harik. He snatches off a taste for himself and then delivers the power to Desh, who gives him permission to cede it to me. How am I doing?"

"Quite well." Then Fingit whispered to Harik, "Drifting Whores! The Murderer is too dangerous to let live. We should kill him as soon as possible."

Harik hissed, "The Murderer is my property. If you touch him, I shall give you to Cheg-Cheg tied up in ribbon."

Fingit shook his head and answered the Murderer. "It's been a while since we've worked a four-cornered deal, but we can certainly manage it. So, Nub, make your offer."

The Murderer began whistling some stupid human melody.

The Nub's face did something between a smile and a grimace. "You should offer me something first. I want something good, and don't try to trick me. Please."

"Murderer, shut the hell up!" Fingit yelled, and the man ceased whistling. "I will deliver, by proxy, two squares of power for the price of—"

The Nub cut in. "Bib, how much power do you need?"

"Two squares are far too much. We need half a square at most."

"I want half a square, Fingit, no more."

The little bastard. That was nothing but luck for him to think of that. Fingit sniffed. "All right. I'll deliver one-half of one square in exchange for the removal of your capability to father children for the rest of your life."

The Nub's mouth dropped open, and he actually covered his groin with one hand. "What? You damned... you..."

The Murderer said, "That is a bit expensive, but understand that Fingit is just taking a tough bargaining position. Desh, as your advisor, I suggest a counteroffer of forgoing one orgasm some time within the next year."

The Nub yelped, "Yes, that one! The orgasm one! That's my offer!"

Fingit put some contempt into his laugh. "That's hardly an offer at all! Did you come here to waste our time? Here's a different offer then. In exchange for the power, you'll become a compulsive gambler with horrible luck."

"No!" the Nub yelled. "Bib? Do you have any advice?"

"Yes, I do, son. I'd offer these snakes one bad but temporary rash in the next year."

"All right... I see what you're saying. I offer one bad but temporary rash in the next year."

Fingit sneered. "Hah! I don't think you came here to bargain at all. Is this a social call? Would you like me to send for refreshments? Here's my counter. I'll give you a nasty mean streak. Not cruel, mind you. Just nasty. How about that?"

"I don't want that!" The Nub was nearly babbling. "Um... I offer having bad penmanship."

"Every woman you ever love will cheat on you."

"Uh, pigs will make me sneeze," the Nub said.

"You'll cheat on every woman you love." Fingit grinned as he played with this new sorcerer.

"I'll forget my wife's anniversary—two years in a row."

"You lose your childhood—all memories gone," Fingit said. *Yes, that's the one. It will bring me a generous reservoir of power, and it'll start toughening up the little biscuit.*

"I... my knee will ache when the weather changes."

"No. All the childhood memories, or no deal."

The Nub turned his head this way and that as if help might come. "This is crazy! Is this really all you'll accept? Bib, can you advise me?"

The Murderer said slowly, "That may be the best deal you'll get, Desh. He knows it's live or die for you."

"How about I just lose my memories of my mother, not the whole childhood?"

"No," Fingit said.

"My mother. That's what I can offer."

Fingit winced. "We can't come to an arrangement then. You may go."

The Murderer shrugged. "Come on, Desh, let's leave."

Is he leaving? They're fading. He's really leaving—Krak's eyeballs! "Wait! Maybe we can arrange something. I'm moved by a young man with such promise."

"So, we have a deal with my memories of my mother?" The Nub chewed his lip.

"Well, no. But for just those memories, I'll offer you one-tenth of a square."

"Desh..." The Murderer shook his head.

"Quiet, Murderer!" Fingit said.

"Bib, can you advise me?" The Nub looked pathetic.

The Murderer gave a slow answer. "Son, one-tenth of a square will heal you, but you'll still lose the leg."

"I... I can't believe this! This is insane! Bib! Damn it to hell and halfway home!"

"Was there an offer somewhere in that rant?" *Come on, just say yes and go back to your horrible life.*

"No! If I ever find that bastard with the spear, I'm going to beat him to death! All right, I'll settle for—"

"Wait!" the Murderer shouted.

"Yes?" The Nub sounded like a puppy waiting for a treat.

"If you're taking the lower offer, hold out for an extra hundredth of a square and keep it for yourself."

"You didn't find some clever trick..."

"Sorry, Desh. Remember, there are no good deals."

The Nub looked down. "I want eleven-hundredths of a square in exchange for all memories of my mother. That's my last offer."

"Impossible!" Fingit snapped.

"Make it possible!" Desh snapped in the same tone.

This is just a fraction of the power I was hoping for. I won't even be able to rebuild my workshop with this. I can't believe it. Fingit whispered, "Harik! This is all your fault! You and your damned sorcerer!"

The God of Death gave Fingit a casual shrug.

Fingit said, "Well... all right, we have a bargain."

"Send a tenth of a square to Bib and the rest to me!" The Nub's voice started trembling.

"Agreed. We could make a separate deal for the leg, you know. An offer you'll like better?"

"No. This is plenty." The Nub's body was sagging a lot for something that has no objective reality.

"We're heading off now." The Murderer grabbed the Nub's spirit again. "We'll let you boys get back to kissing each other's asses."

"Murderer, one more thing," Harik said. "I've extended my offer to cancel your open-ended debt. You may kill the person you most care for anytime within the next week to lift your obligation. The intentional act itself will seal the agreement. Perhaps a good opportunity shall arise."

The humans faded from sight.

"Don't feel bad." Sakaj caressed Fingit's arm as he drew the Nub's power. "You made the first real trade in years. We're witnesses. We know exactly how much you got, just in case Krak asks us."

"Never worry, my fine fellow." Harik patted Fingit's other arm. "I feel certain the Father of the Gods will use all that power sagaciously just as soon as he thrashes you into surrendering it to him."

EIGHT

(Fingit)

*I*f Lutigan flexes his biceps one more time, I'm going to build a
dragon to bite him in half.

Fingit watched the God of War lean back on his marble
throne and flirt with Krak's seminude demigoddess servants.
Sadly, dragon-building was only a dream right now, since Krak
had appropriated almost every drop of power Fingit had squeezed
out of the Nub. That included more than just his spoils from
confiscating the Nub's illusions and taking the memories of his
mother. A few days after the Nub escaped bleeding to death, he
came begging for more power. Fingit had promised the little thug
horrible nightmares. Who snapped all that power up in an
eyeblink? Krak.

Fingit raised his platinum goblet for an angry pull of ambrosia.

*I was the one who got everybody to Unicorn Town. I was the
one who bargained with that little walking sausage of a sorcerer. I
was the one who brought in the power. And this is what Krak does
with it.*

Krak had proclaimed that the highest possible priority was to rebuild his sanctuary, the Temple of Lordly Penetration. The original temple had been built on a scale Krak thought fitting for the divine master of all existence, and it had enclosed more land than a god could comfortably circumnavigate between breakfast and lunch. It stood seventy stories high amid the Towering Mountains of Unfathomable Might, and it rested upon the slopes of the tallest peak, Mount Humility.

As an interior decorator, Krak had always balanced magnificence with austerity. He had filled the stark and elegant white marble structure with grottos of weeping simplicity, each containing a still pool of water, three stunted trees, a vase holding one brilliant dahlia, and a few butterflies in masculine hues. Artful entertainment halls blended into elegant seating and then into simple gardens, with walls adorned by no more than two tasteful paintings. Fingit had always suspected that those gracious living spaces stood atop underground warrens housing an extensive staff of demigods and imps. Those beings were probably packed into quarters that would make a cyanide-filled salt mine seem luxurious.

The original Temple of Lordly Penetration had been the grandest structure in the Home of the Gods, and therefore in all of existence. Cheg-Cheg had crushed it in an afternoon. The monster hadn't left too many of the marble blocks still touching. In fact, he had eaten a surprising quantity of the marble and then deposited semi-digested marble all over the Gods' Realm in piles that inspired both awe and horror.

The new Temple of Lordly Penetration was an opulent two-story villa just large enough to house six egotistical gods. Krak had included gold fixtures and floors inlaid with rich woods, which protected everyone within it from insanity. He had also deemed it wise to place an eighteen-foot-tall statue of himself in the foyer.

Fingit glanced at the marble effigy and then at his father. *What a chunk of nose filth.*

Just two things prevented Fingit from calling Krak a son of a bitch and walking out. First, Krak had fashioned the walls so that they would be invisible to three-hundred-foot-tall monsters. Just that morning, Cheg-Cheg had passed within spitting distance, which for him was about a mile, and never glanced at the temple. Second, before Krak did anything else with Fingit's power, he had siphoned off enough to regain control of the impossibly searing light of the sun. He hadn't yet mastered it the way he had in the old times, but he could certainly burn off an arm or leg when a god got too snotty.

Fingit took another drink. Despite his rage, he had yearned for ambrosia during the years of deprivation. Lutigan was still working to get those demigoddesses off into a discreet alcove. Harik was attempting to engage the God of War in an intellectual discourse on some pretentious crap or other, but Lutigan responded only one time in twelve. In the meantime, Harik sipped ambrosia and nibbled wedges of tin apple. Maybe golden apples would make a resurgence someday, or at least silver ones.

Sakaj sat on her marble throne as if it were a cocoon. Her black hair fell luscious around her shoulders, and she wore a simple red gown with no jewelry. She had pulled her knees up to her chest and folded her bare arms around them, and her eyes flicked from one fellow god to another.

The mighty Father of the Gods rose like a whale and placed his palms on the gleaming black table, which had been formed from a single piece of onyx. He looked virile and strong, but Fingit could see a little tremble in the hands and a bit of a gut on the old fellow. Krak cleared his throat. "Children, we stand on the first step of the stairway that will return us to glory. Man has suffered without our protection and guidance. We have now battered through the barriers so that we may return to mankind, and to our obligations. We have behaved as less than gods, and we have lagged in our duty. But now we will grasp once again the power to defend and nurture mankind as our destiny demands." Krak lifted his diamond goblet. "To our destiny!"

The other gods jumped up and repeated the toast with their golden goblets upraised.

"And to mankind too, of course," Krak added as he dried his lips with a napkin. "Sit, everyone! Now that that's out of the way, what do we do about Cheg-Cheg? We must make plans."

Don't you mean it's time for you to tell the serfs what you want them to do according to the plans you've already made? You clever old son of the Black Drifting Whores of the Universe.

Fingit looked down and wondered whether that was an insult or the literal truth. Then he banned even the tiniest sign of discontent from his expression.

Krak leaned forward. "It all comes down to power. Fingit has struck some respectable bargains with this Nub fellow, and well done, Fingit. Of course, since the Nub is new to all this, I was expecting a more favorable outcome, but it's still nothing to be ashamed of." Krak nodded at Fingit, while Harik sniffed and Lutigan sneered.

"Now, let's sum up our progress!" Krak rubbed his hands together. A flicker of impossibly bright light showed through his fingers as he rubbed them. Every other god at the table froze into polite attention. "Gorlana has discovered a few opportunities. She's found three minor healers—none worth naming—but they've all taken the standard 'village healer deal.' In case any of you have forgotten during your insanity, that's a trickle of power as needed in exchange for a long life of personal suffering and misery, ending as a horrible crone who's burned by the people she spent her life helping. Nothing fancy there, but I'm sure you'll agree that it's a nice start."

The Goddess of Mercy waved a hand in acknowledgment.

Krak nodded toward the God of War. "Lutigan drew a little good luck. He found some awful thug of a bandit with a bit of an aptitude for sorcery. Oddly, the little toad didn't want the standard deal. He wanted wishes!" All the gods laughed hard. "Where do people get these ideas? Wishes indeed! Anyway, he accepted an unknown number of opportunities to make himself unseen by his enemies, in exchange for an agonizing death when his power fails at the most inopportune moment imaginable. Nice work, Lutigan."

Lutigan smiled and flexed his biceps again. Fingit suppressed some insults and indulged a brief fantasy that included a thousand bunnies hurling a net over the mighty Lutigan, dragging him down, and chewing out his heart. And his brain, if they could find the withered thing, banging around inside his skull.

Krak tapped the table with a sound like a lead pipe whacking granite. "Harik has stumbled onto an astounding bit of luck. One of his pre-Veil sorcerers still lives, against all probability. Harik has contacted this Farmer and tells me the man is stuffed with potential trades. His brutality makes the Murderer look like a child that's been running around kicking people in the shin. Harik is even updating the Farmer on the Murderer's movements, so I doubt we'll have to put up with the Murderer's smart-ass comments much longer.

"Fingit, as I said, is cultivating the Nub full time, and we should see a nice return on that over the next couple of years. And Sakaj... well, we all know that deals involving the unknowable are challenging. But when they pay off, they're the most profitable of all. Keep searching, my dear. I understand that the Freak has probably played out, but more opportunities are hiding out there. Never doubt it!"

Sakaj smiled and nodded at Krak with her eyes cast down.

Krak lowered his voice and let his smile dissolve. "Now that we've created this sanctuary of sanity, our highest priority is to increase and stabilize our inflow of resources so we can rebuild our strength." Everyone nodded. "I see two possibilities. We could bring the rest of the gods into our plans."

No one around the table moved. A few eyes shifted back and forth. Fingit assumed that no one wanted to speak in case it might encourage someone else to support this idea. Obviously, they should save all their fellow gods from insanity and degradation, and they would. Perhaps just not quite yet.

Harik stared at the table. "Would we be bringing in... Trutch as well?"

Krak coughed. "Well, if we bring in everyone, then of course your wife would be one of them."

"Ah. I suggest that's not the best option then."

"Well, I didn't think it was, anyway." Krak smiled. Everyone around the table nodded and made noises of agreement. "We six should focus on breaking through to the world of man from this side. Then we won't have to go to Unicorn Town—damn it, Fingit, now you've got me doing it! We won't have to go to the Dark Lands to make deals. We won't have to commit suicide every day, either, and frankly I'm tired of elevating myself. If we can work deals from here without all this suicide and Dark Lands business, our production could go up by an order of magnitude."

After construction had begun on the Temple of Lordly Penetration, Krak had considered how the gods might improve the quality of the deals struck in Unicorn Town. He concluded that their greatest problem was that they no longer enjoyed the advantage of home territory. All of the gods found Unicorn Town to be creepy, and that distracted them during negotiations. To overcome this disadvantage, Krak had created within Unicorn Town a small replica of the gods' traditional trading arena, including the great marble gazebo, the nourishing sunlight, and the bare patch of dirt on which sorcerers would stand to be duped and derided. The structure filled a space no bigger than a ballroom. While the landscapes of forest and fields were just painted on the walls, the sense of familiarity made a difference.

Krak paused and then raised his arms. "So, our path forward is decided!"

Fingit nodded just like everyone else. *About what I expected. Krak drives the wagon to market, and the wee piggies do what they're told. Even if they are divine wee piggies of radiant might.*

Krak stood. "From this point on, there will be no expenditure of resources. None at all! Not so much as a new tiara, resurrecting an extinct animal for a pet, or a shot of overnight virility. Nothing! We hoard any and all resources that come in. Once we have enough, we'll make a push at piercing the Veil."

No one leaped up and cheered Krak's plan, but no one objected out loud, either. Fingit understood that any unhappy soldiers would soon be out there with the other crazy gods, minus a limb or two. They bent their heads and accepted their father's will.

"Follow me then!" Krak ordered. He walked around the table to the far wall, where six wooden chairs stood, each polished to a luster one could almost drink. Above each chair hung a silk noose attached to a beam overhead. Krak climbed upon his chair and began arranging a noose around his neck. Fingit followed Gorlana, Lutigan, and Harik, who were climbing onto their chairs.

"Wait," Sakaj whispered from Fingit's shoulder. "Stay a few moments. I need to talk to you alone."

Fingit glanced at Sakaj, who winked. *I can't think of a single good thing that can come from staying. But if I don't stay, I guess I'll never know.*

A minute later, Krak commanded everyone to leap off his or her chair. A minute after that, four gods hung dead from the beam, while Fingit and Sakaj stood on their chairs and stared past the bodies at each other.

"This feels a lot more awkward than I thought it would," Sakaj said as she reached out to stop her father's body from swinging.

NINE

(Fingit)

Fingit followed Sakaj onto Krak's second-floor balcony that overlooked the Vale of Dominating Perfection. Nostalgia swirled around him as the sun touched the farther mountain peaks.

Before the Veil fell, the gods' home had sprawled beneath an ineffable golden sun of heartrending beauty. After the fall, that sun devolved to a yellow sun of elegant allure, and then a pale, dusty sun of wholesome charm. Later, it shifted to an orange sun of adequate inoffensiveness, and eventually, it became a burnt-umber sun that could be said to at least have a good personality.

Fingit leaned against the rail and appreciated today's sunset of plum, magenta, goldenrod, scarlet, nutmeg, and periwinkle. He estimated that since power began flowing back into the Gods' Realm, sunsets had regained a good 25 percent of their pre-Veil glory.

Maybe it's closer to twenty-seven percent. Can I determine what the precise sunset-glory-recapture factor is? I'd need some lenses and a lot of copper wire. Fingit slipped into an engineer's reverie as schematics and power ratios flowed through his mind.

Sakaj's hand slipped onto Fingit's shoulder from behind, wrinkling his new white robe woven from the hair of the finest sacrificial goats. Sakaj had snapped Fingit's train of thought, but he maintained his poise. He was a god, and a god would never do anything so prosaic as to jump in surprise. He did bite his tongue quite sharply, however, which made him angry with himself and with Sakaj. He used a long, deliberative pause to give his tongue time to recover before he spoke. "Everyone seems happy, eh?"

Sakaj stepped back and nodded, staring into his eyes.

"Are you happy?" Fingit asked, more from politeness than from any real interest in her happiness.

Sakaj shook her head, still staring.

Fingit glared at her. "Hell, you're not going to stop talking and start knocking yourself off again, are you? Because that shit loses its amusement value real quick."

Sakaj smiled with obvious warmth. "No, I'm not going to do that."

Fingit felt a bit sorry that he'd spoken so harshly. "What are you unhappy about then? We're on the road to glory and comfort and power and victory over our indestructible enemy. We're back!"

Sakaj shrugged. "I'll be damned if I sit by and let those demented back-warts take all the glory for themselves. You heard Krak." She clenched her fists and strutted around the room like a constipated gorilla, dropped her voice two octaves, and mouthed each word as if it could fill a cavern with her magnificence. "'Nice job with the pissant village healers! Cultivate this warlord like he was a broccoli stalk! Sakaj's bunch takes a long time to find, but oh, they'll be worth it!' Screw Krak and all the rest of those pathetic, self-congratulating invertebrates."

Fingit looked around, expecting Krak—or a searing beam of light—to hurtle through the door right away.

Sakaj paid him no attention. "Every one of those immortal turd-eaters gave up. They all gave up except for you and me. You hung on to your sanity, which probably makes you the least imaginative and most boring god that's ever existed." Fingit began to object, but Sakaj pushed on. "And I persisted even when I was as crazy as a bug in a butter churn. Those bastards down there didn't elevate themselves hundreds of times to discover how to reach across the Veil. They didn't figure out how to get you over there to help them. I did those things! Who the hell do those cheap paper gods think they are?"

Sakaj's eyes crackled with divine lightning, and her cheeks flared as red as her gown. With her chin up and her breath quick, Fingit became aware that Sakaj was exceedingly attractive—when she was clean and not dismembered, and her hair didn't look like something pulled out of a yak's ass.

"But, what can you do about it?" Fingit asked, covering up his sudden interest in Sakaj's charms. "Krak has spoken. He's told us how things will be. That's the way it is. You know that. Unless you want your breasts to get a tan that goes all the way down to your ribcage?"

Sakaj laughed. "No, I don't intend to get one of those. Effla didn't heal for a month after Krak chastised her bosom off. But I will damned well elevate myself every day for another year before I let any of those smirking, gloating creatures back there snatch even a grain of glory." Sakaj took a step toward Fingit and placed her hand on his chest.

Oh, I am such a dimwit... she knows. She knows I've got a little thing for her, and now she's going to lead me around by the metaphorical dick just because I'm stupid and she can do it. Fingit cleared his throat. "What's your plan?"

"The Freak. We need her to make some deals. None of the other sorcerers can give us as much power as the Freak."

"But isn't she used up? No longer interested?"

"They're always interested, if you offer them the right deal at the right time. You know that. We just have to create those circumstances. I am damn well going to get her to deal."

Fingit chewed his lip. Sakaj grasped the front of his robe and shook it lightly. "We can do it, but I need your help. The Freak now protects her brother's sons, the last of her family's line. The Nub has attracted the love of a river spirit that will do anything to save him from harm. So, you will betray the Nub and give him to his enemies. I will promise the spirit to help her save the Nub, but only if she threatens to kill the Freak's nephews. Then I will force the Freak to bargain with me in order to save those children. She always was soft for children."

Fingit crossed his arms. "That plan's too simple. Would you like to add a cavalry charge and an erupting volcano for spice?"

Sakaj waved Fingit away. "You're adorable. It is not too complex for gods. Kingdoms have been won with plans far more complex.

"What if somebody kills the Nub? Then I've got nothing!"

Sakaj walked to Fingit and stared at him from a foot away. "I won't let that happen. Trust me, the river spirit can slaughter any number of ruffians when my power is with her."

Fingit shook his head, and Sakaj grabbed his jaw. "It will take both of us. But when we push through the Veil using the power that you and I secured, then Harik and the rest will gag on their envy." She put her lips by Fingit's ear and whispered, "And I guarantee that Krak will never forget what we did."

Sakaj released Fingit and stepped back. She crossed her arms over the elegant flash of her cleavage, cocked one svelte hip, tilted her head so that her black hair brushed her bare shoulder, and said, "So?"

She let her question dangle until Fingit was ready to answer. After a good thirty seconds, he sighed. "All right. How do we do this?"

(Sakaj)

By the time Krak's servants had lit all the lanterns, Sakaj had educated Fingit on her plan. Then she grew tired of his mumbling, head-shaking, and repeated questions, so she sent him away to hang himself. She patted his cheek and promised to be right behind him, just to take the sting out.

No matter what she told that nearsighted tinkerer, Sakaj's plans balanced on the point of failure. Perhaps that was generous. Her plans were rushing like a waterfall into a lagoon of putrefaction. But she refused to surrender and let that bucket of walrus drool Harik, or that walking scrotum-with-a-sword Lutigan, drape himself in glory.

Sakaj suspected that assistance might be as close as whispering a plea for help. But that kind of help would be worse than her current problems. As a god, she hated to admit that she'd done the kind of ignorant thing she'd seen so many mortals do. But she had, and she'd better admit it, at least to herself. She had no room now for self-deception.

Eight years ago, as the most recent War of Shattering Woe was just ending, Sakaj found herself alone one day in the Dim Lands. Cheg-Cheg had elevated her by smothering her in his armpit on the final day of the war. At that time, the Dim Lands were as beautiful in their way as the Home of the Gods. Sakaj was dangling her feet in the River of Regret, coaxing fish to jump out of the water for her, when a cultured voice rumbled, "I'm awfully sorry about the armpit. It was a necessity of war, but still, I'm certain it lacked charm."

Sakaj whipped about to see all three hundred feet of Cheg-Cheg blotting out the sky above her. Shock crashed through her brain, since previously Cheg-Cheg's most articulate statement had been vomiting a battered chariot. He now ran his hideous, eviscerating talons across the tops of the trees as a gentleman might primp a flower arrangement.

Sakaj was a goddess who prided herself on being imperturbable. As the Mistress of the Unknowable, she also prided herself on being inscrutable. Therefore, when she squeaked like a girl whose pigtail had been pulled, she felt a bit embarrassed.

Cheg-Cheg demonstrated the good manners to ignore her squeak of surprise. "You have a beautiful spot here. It exudes loveliness. I shall be sad when I someday lay waste to it and befoul the earth so that nothing may ever grow here again."

Sakaj stood tall and calmed her breathing. "That would be a shame. You could just, oh, forget to do it. Let it slip your mind."

"Perhaps." Cheg-Cheg gazed at the prismatic sun and the clouds of shifting colors.

"I've never seen you here before," Sakaj said, pushing her hair back. "I didn't think anyone could come here except gods, to tell you the truth."

Cheg-Cheg glanced down at her before saying, "Oh, that's not true. Not true at all. They call me the Dark Annihilator of the Void and Vicinity, correct?"

Sakaj nodded.

"Well, this"—Cheg-Cheg gestured around, obliviously cutting three massive blue gum trees in half—"is a Vicinity." He peered down, and streamers of drool that burned like acid ran from his fangs. "I just wanted to pop in here for a brief visit before I set off into the Void. This place rather refreshes my soul, if you understand me."

"I do understand you." And then Sakaj did a stupid thing. She started thinking. She said, "If you travel between the Vicinities and the Void, you must know a lot about what separates different places."

"I certainly do." Cheg-Cheg tested the river with one claw of his nightmarish foot. "I travel them all when the mood strikes. I daresay no one knows the pathways better."

"Well, I've always wondered... rather idly... about the separation—" Sakaj's statement sliced off mid-sentence when an astounding noise flattened her to the ground.

"I'm so sorry," Cheg-Cheg said as Sakaj crawled to her feet. "I couldn't help laughing. Let me guess. You want to know what connects you to the world of mankind."

"Um, yes." Sakaj nodded. "We have some theories—"

"Ribbon of cloth," Cheg-Cheg interrupted her. "That's the right one. Although some of your other theories are terribly amusing. I particularly love the one about the tunnel. It's so grotesque."

Sakaj's mind whirled. She now had the answer to an ages-old question. More importantly, only *she* had the answer. Then she did the truly stupid, ignorant, and moronic thing. "Would it be possible to, ah, affect the ribbon at all?"

"Most certainly."

Sakaj held her breath. *My children are valuable, but they've always been rare. Most humans are too obtuse to understand me. If I could alter the ribbon just a bit to help other sorcerers see my glory, I could make so many more trades. And get so much more power. Just a little tweak...*

Sakaj explained her desire to Cheg-Cheg, and he agreed to help her with no more fuss than handing her a pebble from the ground. He explained that the sky there in the Dim Lands provided one of the closer connections between the realms, so that's where the work should be done. She could accomplish her goal by washing the ribbon itself.

To Sakaj's horror, Cheg-Cheg thrust a talon into the back of his appalling maw and dug out something white about the size of her head. He dropped it to her. She feared it would be part of someone he ate, but instead, it was a tough, head-size egg, warm to touch.

Cheg-Cheg instructed Sakaj to crack the egg and fling its contents into the sky, but he cautioned her to first wash herself with rigorous attention to the tiniest soil or stain. Any contamination could throw the wash awry, and the ribbon might not turn out as intended. Sakaj disrobed and bathed herself in the River of Regret, paying closest attention to her hands. Then with Cheg-Cheg watching, she broke open the egg and hurled its pearl-white contents into the sky. The jet of whiteness shot away and disappeared into the clouds.

"How will we know if it's working?" Sakaj asked a few moments later.

Cheg-Cheg yawned. "A gentle white snowfall will be your sign. It should arrive just... about... now."

Enormous snowflakes began wafting down through the still air of the Dim Lands. Sakaj caught one, and she saw that it was pink.

Despite her fear of Cheg-Cheg, Sakaj screamed at him, "What did you do? What's wrong?"

Cheg-Cheg sniffed. "I did nothing wrong. You must have contaminated the wash. It must have bled."

Sakaj gaped at the monster. Then she looked at her hands and saw a drop of blood on her left palm. She must have cut it on the eggshell.

"Well, that will have some unintended consequences, I'll bet," Cheg-Cheg rumbled. Then he looked hard at the goddess. "Really, you should know better. Upon how many humans have you perpetrated these very sorts of shenanigans? Now I must go. I shall assail your land again the next time I happen to wander by. Perhaps I shall destroy you utterly next time. I do enjoy my little visits with your people. Say hello to your father for me." With a final caress of the trees, Cheg-Cheg faded out of the Dim Lands.

That was how Sakaj had caused the Veil to fall, and she'd been laboring ever since to fix things. And she would damn well be boiled like a shrimp and served to Cheg-Cheg on a cracker before she let anyone else take credit for the work she had put in to fixing this unholy mess.

Sakaj suspected that if she called out to Cheg-Cheg from the Dim Lands right then, he might answer, and that if he answered, he might offer help. But she had not yet reached the crisis of desperation that would lead her back to Cheg-Cheg for assistance.

Sakaj sighed and padded back downstairs to her waiting noose.

TEN

"Make it rain toads for me. Or even better, porpoises."
"I can't even make it rain water." Fingit grimaced at Sakaj as they lay side by side on the black grass.

"Well, raise a volcano then. These sorcerers are less interesting than mud. I miss the old days when we could just make things happen to people."

Fingit ignored that and gazed back up at the Unicorn Town sky with its window onto mankind. There he saw the Nub and his river spirit, arguing among some rocks on a mountain slope. It was at least a three-day journey through these mountains, because Fingit and Sakaj had watched them walk across rocks and gravel for three soul-numbing days.

"I almost wish Cheg-Cheg would try to kill us again." Sakaj yawned.

"Huh." Fingit heard the pout in her voice. Four days ago, Cheg-Cheg had roared into Unicorn Town, forcing the gods to flee by jumping back home. The beast had snatched Lutigan and was lifting the God of War to his mouth just as Lutigan aban-

87

doned his Unicorn Town body. If Lutigan had been a second or two slower, he'd have been destroyed forever.

In that case, I might have thrown a little party. I wonder what kind of gift Cheg-Cheg would like? Fingit chuckled, drawing a frown from Sakaj. *Oh, well, all this useless watching has made me a little irritable too.*

Cheg-Cheg had ignored Unicorn Town since that attack, and Fingit had spent most of his time watching the Nub limp along during the daytime and sleep at night. The boy had created a magical false leg to replace his destroyed one, and it looked like he'd done a handy job, though unsightly. Fingit had also eavesdropped on the young man, whose conversations were less informative than the grunting and vomiting of drunken longshoremen, but without any interesting profanity. The Nub hadn't said anything that gave Fingit good ideas about how to betray the young sorcerer.

"All right." Sakaj sat up. "Describe the situation to me again. What have you found out? And do it in one sentence, you babbler. I do not need to hear how humans first learned to use fire and cover their private bits."

Fingit held back a nasty statement about her being a giant whiner. "The Nub is headed for some awful city to free the Murderer and some woman, although why he wants to do it perplexes me. The Farmer severed the Murderer's hands, thank the nasty Void-beasts for that. That's justice for that foul-mouthed, irreverent sorcerer. He's now a eunuch where magic's concerned, soon to be a corpse where everything's concerned." Fingit glared at Sakaj and waited for her to say something about his using more than one sentence.

Sakaj pressed her lips together, but she said nothing about his long-windedness. "Good. I predicted this. The spirit will not accompany the Nub into that city. Men have laid too many stones one against another for her to bear it. The Nub will therefore ask you for help entering the city. He cannot do it without magic if he expects to save the Murderer, or if he even expects to live."

"The spirit has been telling him to find another way," Fingit said. "She's made the same argument using the same words in the same tone of voice for two days. I wish I could send a hundred lions to eat her."

"Stay focused. Betray the Nub, and I'll send the spirit after those children. Then the Freak will trade us a lake of power, I'll help the spirit save the Nub, and you will still have the Nub to squeeze until he's a flaky husk."

Sakaj lay back down beside Fingit, and in silence they watched the Nub and his river spirit walk and walk and walk.

When sunset scraped across the world of man, it turned the mountain valley hazy or stark by turns, depending on the shadows. The Nub and his river spirit stopped for the evening, made camp, and began preparing a meal for the young sorcerer.

Fingit nudged Sakaj. "I wish there was something to eat here. Or that we could bring something with us."

"How do you know we can't bring things with us? Have you tried? I haven't."

Fingit didn't argue, nor did he ask her how she thought it could be done. The Smith of the Gods didn't think that way. He instead started analyzing how to do it, and whether he had everything he needed to do it.

When the world of man had become as dark as Unicorn Town, Fingit chuckled. "Would you like some soup?"

"What? Don't you dare!"

But Fingit had already released his body, and after some interval of unconsciousness, he was reborn in the Home of the Gods. He ran to the tiny blue cottage he'd built to replace his lovely, now-vaporized home. Then he clattered around in the obsessively organized kitchen for a while before packing a dragon-skin bag with a sealed clay jug of leviathan-coriander soup. He also packed golden bowls and platinum spoons. He might have been a pauper by divine standards, but he still had some self-respect.

His suicide by hanging felt a little hurried, and the rope was scratchy, but it did the job. Fingit awoke in Unicorn Town, close to his abandoned body. He hadn't gotten accustomed to that creepy phenomenon.

Unicorn Town had forced the gods to reconsider how their bodies existed. Before then, only two places mattered: the Home of the Gods and the Dim Lands. Whenever a god was elevated, he awoke in the Dim Lands with all the injuries and mutilations he had suffered during elevation. He would be trapped there until the next sunrise. Then he'd be reborn with a perfect body in the Home of the Gods, and his corpse would disappear at the same time.

Throughout the ages, the gods recognized in a desultory way that while elevated, they had two bodies: a lifeless corpse in the Home of the Gods, and an identical but animated body in the Dim Lands. They knew that this probably meant something, possibly something important. However, nobody ever saw his own lifeless corpse, so the gods figured they shouldn't poke around with things that weren't broken.

Unicorn Town seemed to work just like the Dim Lands at first. If a god was elevated while thinking about Unicorn Town as a destination, he awoke in Unicorn Town with all his wounds. But then Sakaj screwed the whole thing up by figuring out how to jump out of Unicorn Town and be reborn back home without waiting for sunrise.

Now a god could be elevated at home, wake up in Unicorn Town, jump back home, wake up in a perfect body, and literally trip over his own corpse. He could elevate himself again and wake up beside the body he left behind in Unicorn Town. If he did this over and over, he could theoretically populate a life-size model of an entire gala ball, or the Battle of the Whaling Balladeers, with nothing but his own corpses. If the gods survived the current war, at some point they would do exactly those things. They would do things far more inventive, elaborate, and horrible. Eternity is long.

All corpses in all realms disappeared at sunrise. Every other being in existence should have offered thanks for that, since it saved them from discovering what the gods would do with millions of their own corpses.

Fingit walked a wide circle around his corpse to reach Sakaj. Then he pulled the jar of soup out of the dragon-skin bag suspended by a silk strap over his shoulder.

"You're crazier than me!" Sakaj shouted. "What is wrong with you? The opportunity might have arisen and you would have missed it!"

"Did the opportunity arise?"

"No," Sakaj grumbled.

Fingit raised the jar over his head. "Then we have soup!"

They sat a polite distance away from Fingit's body and unpacked the bag. Sakaj blew on the soup. "It's mere luck that you didn't miss anything important. I have heard murmuring, but nothing loud enough to be distinct."

Fingit bent over his bowl. "Doesn't the soup smell good?"

"Fine! It's good soup. It'll nourish the body and raise the dead. Shut up about it."

"Fingit!" a voice bellowed from the darkness. It reverberated so that Fingit sloshed some hot soup onto his thumb.

"It's the Nub," Fingit whispered. The young man sounded more frightened than he had the last time, and the last time, he'd been bleeding to death. Fingit slipped into the faux trading arena and pulled at the young sorcerer. The Nub materialized on the bare dirt patch. He stared around as if he'd be able to see something. A lot of sorcerers did that.

This is it. Betray the Nub and trust Sakaj to save him, because I sure won't be able to help him.

The gods disapproved of betraying sorcerers. They had no moral objection to it, but it tended to hurt the gods as often as it did the sorcerers. Early in the gods' dealings with men, Harik conceived a clever scheme that involved betraying a sorcerer into a perilous situation, then offering to sell the sorcerer a means of escape that would save him, only to betray him into a worse situation, and so on. He figured he could drain a sorcerer of all possible value in fewer than four days, or fewer than three if the sorcerer lived in a dangerous neighborhood.

The inaugural attempt of this scheme appalled Harik. He found that after the first betrayal, he couldn't even contact the sorcerer, never mind charge an obscene price to save him. The fellow drowned in a sewer, and Harik lost a valuable property.

Trial and error revealed that once a god betrayed a sorcerer, the god could not contact the fellow until he extricated himself. Other gods might speak to the sorcerer, but not the god who committed the betrayal. This phenomenon pissed off all the gods, but Krak declared it was just the universe maintaining balance. He explained, "If you tend a tree, then you may reach up and pick apples every year. But if you cut down the tree so that you don't have to reach up, don't cry next year about not having any damned apples."

All right, I'm going to betray the Nub. Oh, hell, Sakaj is right, I am crazier than she is.

Sakaj kept silent, but she stood nearby.

"Fingit," the Nub said again, in a much calmer tone than before.

"That's better," Fingit replied. "That first scream sounded like an ox being sacrificed with a dull sword. Now that you're here, Nub, what do you want? Not to be brusque, but I left dinner to answer your call, and I don't care to keep my charming escort waiting. So what will it be? Are you tired of the river spirit? Do you want the Murderer's blonde girl to fall in love with you? Love charm, maybe? Do you want an ugly sword to match your sling? Armor that can't be pierced, or a saddle that makes your horse run faster? What will it be?"

The Nub pulled back his shoulders and stood tall. "I don't want any of that crap. I want to make something to disguise myself and three other people."

"Ah, Nub. You're about to do something naughty or something stupid. Probably both. I'd love to guess, but my soup is getting cold. Details, Nub! I can't deal if I don't have details!"

The Nub's voice came back loud and steady. "That's not important. The important thing is that I know what I need, and I want you to make me an offer."

Oh, this shit will never do.

"My goodness, you're a tough negotiator, Nub. Pass my congratulations on to the Murderer. Now go suck on your toes, you rusty speck."

The Nub disappeared as if he were a ball Fingit had hurled away.

"Yes, of course you had to slap him down." Sakaj's voice quavered a little. "He'll come back."

"No doubt. I just had to show him his place. Definitely." After a few seconds, Fingit realized he was still nodding, as if nodding would make it true. He sighed and looked down at the soup. "Well, should we eat while we're waiting?"

The Nub's voice drifted from the blackness. "Fingit! I apologize. Please deal with me."

Fingit winked at Sakaj, and she smiled back. He pulled the voice closer and saw the Nub again. "Now my soup is almost certainly cold. I'm offering you another chance only because of your youth and inexperience. Now, details."

"All right. I need to rescue my friends without getting killed, and I want to make magical disguises. Good ones. I don't want them to blow up."

Fingit whispered to Sakaj, "A disguise? Can we do something to him with a disguise?"

"Maybe," Sakaj whispered. "Could you trade him a disguise that won't work against certain people, or not against animals? We need his enemy to capture him."

Fingit smiled so that the Nub would hear it in his voice. "Well, that's simple enough, I suppose. How much power do you want?"

"I... I don't know."

"How do you plan to make this thing?"

The Nub got quieter. "I don't know that, either."

"What kind of object do you intend to create?"

"I don't know what kind of object it would need to be."

Fingit whispered to Sakaj, "Oh, this is precious. He doesn't know a damned thing. I could sell him an enchanted horse turd that he has to hold between his teeth for as long as he wants to be disguised."

Sakaj suppressed a giggle.

Trying not to laugh, Fingit said, "Do you know anything at all?"

"I have to make it out of cloth or leather, because that's all I've got," the Nub mumbled.

"Hmm. Don't you have some grass and dirt as well?"

"Yes! Will that help?" The Nub sounded as excited as one of those little dogs that jumps on your leg.

"Not even the tiniest bit." Fingit bit his lip and pounded his leg with his fist, and he managed not to guffaw.

The Nub sagged. "So, there's nothing I can do?"

"Well, I don't think that a real sorcerer would give up just because of a few obstacles. I can help you, although it will cost a little more."

"How much more?"

"That all depends on the deal you make. I'll provide you the knowledge to make what you want, as well as the power you need, which is one one-thousandth of a square, by the way. Make me an offer."

The Nub looked around, even though there was nothing to see but the darkness enveloping him. "You make the first offer. Please."

Fingit whispered, "Won't make me an offer. This is that damned Murderer's fault."

"The important thing is what you're going to give him," Sakaj whispered, laying her hand on Fingit's shoulder.

Fingit grabbed her hand. "Are you sure the Freak will trade?"

Sakaj lay her other hand on top of Fingit's. "I promise it. The Nub may get a little bruised, cut, or burned, but he'll live."

"All right," Fingit whispered. "I'll sell him a disguise that will fail just before his enemy comes into view. That'll keep him from getting snatched by the wrong people. Or killed someplace along the way."

Sakaj smiled and squeezed Fingit's hand.

Fingit said, "Nub, I'm in a hurry, so let's not waddle around like walruses on a dance floor. I'll make a good offer, you make your offer, and if we can't make it work, then we'll call this off. Those are my conditions."

The Nub laughed, and it almost sounded convincing. "Make your offer, mighty Fingit."

"You will become the most hated man on this continent." Fingit winked at Sakaj.

The Nub stamped his foot. "Come on, Fingit! Be just a little bit serious, all right?"

"Make your offer to me and make it fast!" *Time pressure. That's what will trip him up.*

"Some dogs won't like me. Small dogs." The Nub held his palm less than a foot off the ground. "For a year."

"How unimaginative. Very well, you won't become the most hated man, but people will dislike you. On every continent."

"Nobody will loan me money for a year," he countered.

Fingit chuckled. "Come on, nobody will loan you money *now*. Random people will despise you for no reason, but only for a year."

The Nub chewed his lip, probably unaware that Fingit was watching him. "They will ignore me, but not despise me."

"Oh, you wish them not to despise you? Fine, maybe they'll just dislike you. Do you think your little feelings can stand it if they dislike you?"

The Nub said, "How about I will dislike—not hate—other people for a month?"

Fingit whispered, "What an idiot! That's a horrible deal."

Sakaj whispered, "Why are you talking to me then?"

Fingit said, "That's a creative offer, Nub. Perhaps you'll dislike them for a year."

"A month."

"Three months?"

The Nub swallowed and looked around with huge eyes. "Done."

"Let it be so. You will know how to make your items when you get back. It was a pleasure doing business with you, although you did ruin my evening."

"I was kind of scared to call you, Fingit, but I figured it would be better than getting killed at the Eastern Gateway." The Nub had no physical body and couldn't perspire, but he tried to wipe sweat off his face anyway.

"You're welcome, Nub. Good luck with this stupid thing you're planning."

The Nub faded from view, leaving Fingit and Sakaj alone again.

Fingit began dribbling the power and knowledge to the Nub. "Well, I did my part. You had better be right about this." Fingit put as much threat into his voice as he could, which wasn't really all that much.

Sakaj said, "I am right, and everything will work out sweetly, as I promised. But why was this such a horrible deal? Surely disliking people is better than them disliking you."

"You would think that, but no. Being disliked is an annoyance, sure. But disliking everybody will eat him from the inside. He may never recover. Well, it is only for three months, so there's a small chance he'll heal."

Sakaj nodded. "You can be a sneaky bastard. I must remember that. Now, I'm ready to concentrate fully on your soup."

ELEVEN

(Fingit)

On the day that the gods would later call the Moment of Transcendent Uncertainty, Sakaj materialized unconscious in Unicorn Town as usual. However, her arrival couldn't be considered entirely routine, since her body was smashed flat like a godly rug two yards in diameter, leaving only her shoulders and head intact. Fingit walked around her several times, musing about what had caused this near-complete annihilation.

When Sakaj opened her eyes, she wriggled, grunted, and then banged her forehead against the grass. She cleared her throat before saying in a breathy voice, "Damn Krak to eat his own toes for eternity!"

"Krak did this?"

"Yes! Sort of. Evidently, the rule about not using any power doesn't apply to His Magnificence. He proclaimed that his stronghold is no more than a 'perilously cramped hovel' that must be shored up for everyone's safety."

"It is a little tight. I could smell Lutigan from across the room."

Sakaj sneered. "Well, to Krak, 'shoring up' means adding a four-story wing that increases the stronghold's size twentyfold."

Is there any rational justification for that? Probably not. Dad's just a power-mad megalomaniac. Which makes sense for the divine ruler of all existence. So, he's getting better.

"Shoring up also means imps swinging enormous marble blocks in all directions, and occasionally dropping one." Sakaj panted as deeply as her squished lungs would allow, which wasn't very deep at all.

Fingit realized upon examining her pulverized, burst-to-pieces gross self that he no longer felt at all attracted to Sakaj. "I think you arrived in time anyway. The Nub is dawdling around in the outer city, and the Farmer is heading toward him at last. They should collide pretty soon, unless one of them gets distracted by a glittery bauble or a rabbit or something like that."

Sakaj strained to look up, but her neck and shoulders stuck up from her pulverized body at a difficult angle. At last, she gave up. "By Krak's middle finger, help me turn my head!"

Fingit adjusted her head. "Ugh. That will be giving me nightmares."

"Be quiet! Look!" Sakaj tried to point with her chin. "The Nub is disguised as a guard!"

"I know that. I sold him the disguise," Fingit said. "Hush! He's walking right toward the Farmer, there, on the other side of that nasty little building."

The Nub had stopped next to a tavern and was staring around like a lost goose. Then he looked at his sleeve and stiffened. His disguise, an enchanted loop of cotton around his wrist, was pulling itself apart for no reason and falling to the ground.

That did it. The disguise has failed. Fingit chewed his lip and then opened his mouth.

"Don't even speak!" Sakaj's head wobbled, but that didn't

diminish her anger. "I'm so tired of hearing you whimper about things that could go wrong. Everything's going perfectly."

Fingit closed his mouth and tried to think victorious thoughts.

The Nub must have realized he was in danger, but he didn't know that danger was walking right toward him. He trotted around the corner into an alley. Then a huge blob of a man hurtled out a door and crashed into the Nub as he was passing. He flew across the alley, hit the far wall, and slid to the ground.

"No! That's not supposed to happen!" Fingit covered his mouth in an ungodlike fashion.

Sakaj hissed, "Wait. Just wait. It will be fine."

Another man stumbled out through the door, and everyone started yelling. Fingit could hear them in perfect detail. The big, tubby man bellowed, "Get out of the way, you shitty little man-whore! Or hell, stay down there, I don't give a damn. I can tup you up or tup you down." He grabbed at his crotch, which repulsed Fingit when he realized the man was drunk and fumbling to take down his trousers.

The Nub stood up and backed away.

"Get back here!" the man bellowed louder, grasping for the young sorcerer.

Three more men clumped out of the building.

Fingit said, "Damn it! Those men will drag the Nub inside and rape him to death!"

Fingit missed the Nub's next words, but the big man swayed and slurred something in response. The Nub pulled a pathetic little knife from his belt.

Sakaj squinted at the window to the world of man. "Are you sure the Nub is a sorcerer? He seems rather puny and breakable to me."

Fingit hissed as the walloping drunkard lurched toward the Nub, but then one of the other men whacked the drunk with a club. He fell like a hailstone. The man with the club said, "Sorry, lad. Will's the sweetest fellow you'd ever meet, except when he's pissed as a loon."

"I'm sure he's a regular plum pudding." The Nub backed away, nodding, smiling, and scanning the alleyway. "Thanks for the help."

Fingit pointed up at the window. "Look! The Farmer is turning the corner!"

"Do you see? Everything will transpire as I foretold it." Sakaj wheezed and panted.

The Farmer paused behind the Nub, cocked his head at the young man, and then kicked the Nub's legs out from under him. A moment later, the Nub's enemy had dragged him up by the collar and slipped a dagger from his belt.

Fingit held his breath. The Nub hung almost limp, writhing no more effectively than a baby. The Farmer raised the dagger and smacked the Nub on the back of the neck with its round pommel. The Nub fell to the ground.

"Perfection!" Sakaj wiggled her head with joy. "Just as I planned."

The Farmer directed some other men to carry the Nub away.

Sakaj grinned. "I'm sure the torturing will begin soon."

Fingit thought Sakaj might have been rubbing her hands together, if she still had hands to speak of. "It does seem to have worked out pretty well."

"Now for the river spirit." The Goddess of the Unknowable shifted the window back into the mountains where the river spirit paced back and forth in a manner most unlike a supernatural being. "Spirit, attend me. You are called by She-Who-Must-Not-Be-Named." Sakaj's words flowed from her thoughts, clear and resonant.

The blue spirit, in the perfect form of a woman, appeared without delay. "Yes, Mighty Goddess?" Water dripped from her, and her hair floated above her shoulders. As her breath came quicker, the water droplets fell slower and slower until they hung in midair.

"Your little sorcerer boy is about to be tortured to death in that city."

The spirit paled two shades of blue.

Sakaj said, "I will help you save him if you perform a service for me. Two hundred miles from here, at the headwaters of the Fead River, two boys are lost in the woods. When I give you leave, you must kill them. Make it brutal. Wait until I give you a signal. Do you understand?"

"Yes," the spirit said in a calm voice, but her hands were shaking.

"You may go."

The spirit left so quickly she almost seemed to disappear.

"Now I shall present these facts to the Freak and strike a deal with her." Sakaj closed her eyes, tried to take a breath, and gagged when her half-inch-thick lungs refused. She wheezed a curse and gazed upward. The window in the sky above her swirled and swept for nearly a minute. Then it settled on a rude camp in the lee of a brilliant stand of maple trees. A tall, rangy woman with deep-black skin handed two dead rabbits to a bald, fat man and then squatted beside a campfire.

Sakaj said in a nurturing voice, "Daughter."

The Freak sat up like a prairie dog. She flipped back her dark-brown braid and gazed around. She was a beautiful woman, not yet middle-aged. "No. Leave me alone. I have nothing for you. No deals."

Sakaj grinned and whispered, "She's resisting me. I forgot how cute she can be sometimes." Sakaj closed her eyes. Several seconds went by as her grin devolved into a grimace. At last, she snapped, "You come here right now, young lady!"

The Freak formed from a bank of darkness. She stood a head taller than most men in this part of the world. "What?"

Sakaj wiggled her shoulders lovingly. "Is that any way to greet your mother?"

"You are not my mother. That is a game you play. You do not call me Daughter—you call me Freak."

Sakaj poured love into her voice. "But you *are* my daughter. My favorite daughter." She winked at Fingit.

The Freak laughed, but it was as humorous as a slap in the face. "You called for me, so say what you want. I was about to pick my nose on the other side. I don't want to wait, since that is infinitely more important than this."

Fingit whispered, "Why do you let her talk to you that way? You're as bad as Harik."

Sakaj ignored him and spoke out loud to the Freak. "Fine. Now that our reunion is past, I must bring a distressing issue to your attention. Your little friends—your brother's boys—have become lost and will be murdered before the day ends."

The Freak blinked twice. "I find that unlikely."

"Because your father attends them? Because he carries a bone enchanted by Fingit? You know how Fingit is. He builds flying chariots that crash; he makes impervious armor that causes impotence. Failure is inevitable."

Fingit whispered, "That's not fair at all! That armor wasn't my fault. I didn't know the steel had been mined in the Harpy Mountains!"

Sakaj showed Fingit her teeth. "Hush. It's a bargaining tactic. You mewl like an infant sometimes."

The Freak almost smiled. "Failure or success. They mean nothing to me. Kill them or not."

Sakaj whispered, "Shit."

"What? What?" Fingit dropped to his knees in front of her.

"Nothing! I just cleared my throat," Sakaj whispered. Then she spoke to the Freak. "Well, dear, perhaps you don't care at all about those children. But another boy will soon be tortured, and that boy knows my name. He will talk. One cannot doubt that."

Fingit glared at Sakaj. Speaking the Goddess of the Unknowable's name ranked as the second worst thing a sorcerer could do. Such an act invited Sakaj into the world of man. During her visits, Sakaj always killed at least ten thousand people, and no visitation could be complete without destroying a major city or two. She sometimes left behind poisoned or haunted places that continued to kill and maim once she had departed.

The *worst* thing a sorcerer could do was put a magical object inside a magical creature in a magical location—also known as the "Stuff a Wand at the Standing Stones Blunder." As an example, a foolish sorcerer might lure a fairy or troll to the Majestic Standing Stones of Lipp and then place a magic wand inside the creature in some expeditious manner.

While all celestial and numerological indicators said that this would grant fabulous power, in fact every one of the sorcerer's progenitors would be instantly and retroactively destroyed going back a thousand years. That would snuff out the sorcerer in a handy fashion. It would also wipe out a colossal swath of human beings descended from any of those who had been eliminated.

A sorcerer first committed this error in the distant past. It remained a cautionary tale until another ambitious sorcerer attempted it again just six hundred years ago. She achieved the same result, which says a lot about mankind's ability to pay attention.

Fingit grabbed Sakaj's jaw and whispered, "The Nub knows your name? Really? You couldn't have said something?"

"Of course he doesn't know it!" she whispered.

The Freak didn't answer. She stood motionless.

"But you, my dear daughter," Sakaj murmured, "you can prevent all of this carnage. Only you can forestall it. Don't you feel the tiniest bit of responsibility?"

Again, the Freak kept silent.

"You can stop it. I offer you power. Destroy your enemies, save your family, and seal off this horrible, world-rending knowledge. All you have to do is make an offer."

After a long pause, the Freak said, "I will make you this offer. I wish for you to have vengeful termites infest every opening in your body—yes, including that one. I wish for you to hear the screams of your dying children. I wish for you to weep for ten thousand years. That is my only offer to you."

"What? You will condemn your own kin?" Flecks of spit flew as Sakaj shouted. "You'll risk thousands of deaths, or hundreds of thousands? When you could save them?"

"Let them die. I have nothing left that I will trade." The Freak faded out of the arena.

"What the hell's going on?" Fingit beckoned as if that might bring the woman back.

Back on the plains in the human world, Fingit heard the fat man say, "What the hell's going on?"

The Freak said, "My mother just visited me. The boys have been killed. My mother meant for me to think there's time to save them so that I would trade with her. But they are dead. When I denied her, she made up some ridiculous story about a boy revealing her name."

Fingit glared at Sakaj and shouted, "Wow, you really foretold the hell out of that, didn't you?"

Sakaj's head dropped forward and flopped around. She howled, "That shouldn't have happened! She should have made the deal! Her entire life points to her making that deal!"

"Well, she didn't! Who's going to save the Nub now? Maybe I should bring Harik into this. He can get the Murderer to save the Nub."

"Do not dare go to Harik!" Sakaj said. "If you get anyone else involved, I will find ways for you to suffer that the universe has never seen."

"Well... the Murderer doesn't have hands, anyway." Fingit thought about that for a moment. He realized he was pouting and reset his lips into a hard line. "What do you suggest we do now?"

"Let's keep watching. I'll think of something." Sakaj cleared her throat and panted for a while.

Fingit plopped onto the grass near Sakaj's head. *I deserve this. I did what I've seen so many humans do. I let my penis lead me down the path of destruction. What an idiot.*

TWELVE

(Fingit)

Fingit stood over the flattened Sakaj in Unicorn Town. "I'm telling Krak about every willful, disobedient, ridiculous thing you've done since... ever since you were born!"

"You will be right in the tale with me, brother. Everything will work out. Just watch."

The Nub had been kidnapped fewer than twenty minutes before. The young sorcerer's head still flopped around as the Farmer's men carried him through the sad, human buildings. They took him into one side of a squalid, rotting wooden structure and through to a yard on the other side.

The Farmer, a short, ice-pale, black-haired man, frowned at the Nub. "Louze, attend to the leg."

One of the men, squatty and long-armed, removed the Nub's false leg and tossed it onto a disintegrating woodpile thirty feet away. Then the Farmer directed that the Nub be tied to some kind of brightly painted wooden scaffold. Wildflowers and children's playthings dotted the nearby grass, including a yellow ball and a gaily painted wooden porpoise the size of a stout raccoon.

"Seems awfully cheery for torture," Fingit said.

"Perhaps he's a poor torturer. An amateur."

The Farmer grunted and waved. Louze ripped off the Nub's shirt. An old man brought two buckets of water, and Louze tossed both into the young man's face one after the other. The Nub's head rolled a bit.

"You're awake. How delightful." The Farmer gave a little smile and rubbed the stubble on his jaw with the back of his hand. "I thought I might have to send for a third bucket of water. We've not been formally introduced. I am Vintan Reth. What is your name, sir?"

"Desh Younger," the Nub croaked.

"Lovely! And did that miserable chunk of flesh you once called a leg have any other names before we destroyed it?" The Farmer stepped close to examine the Nub's squinting eyes.

Louze snickered. The Nub didn't answer.

"Before we say anything else, I must extend my deepest apologies. I couldn't find a proper dungeon, and I had to make do."

The Nub glanced around at the gentle scene.

"I know, it's terribly improper. Not even any mold." The Farmer hmphed. "Apparently, no one tortures anymore..."

Fingit whined, "If this torturing is just a slap-dash affair, he may kill the Nub prematurely. I don't like this."

"Stop!" Sakaj put as much power into the word as her smashed-flat lungs could manage. "By the sucking sounds of the Void, shut up! It will be fine. I promise. Look how abashed and contrite the torturer is about these circumstances. I'm certain he will take all possible precautions."

The Farmer was saying, ". . . does lead us here, for which I must again apologize. I am truly sorry that you will be tortured to your shrieking death while strapped to a child's plaything."

The Nub said, "Try not to get any blood on this thing. You might upset the children."

"Shrieking death?" Fingit pointed up at the Nub and glared at Sakaj. "He said shrieking death!"

Sakaj pursed her lips. "Hyperbole."

The Farmer smiled. "Thank you. I misjudged you, Desh. You're the kind of man it's a pleasure to torture. I regret that I will be busy elsewhere soon, but you can feel well cared for since I am leaving Louze with you." The Farmer nodded at his near-simian henchman.

Louze stepped close to the Nub, reached up, and broke the young man's left thumb. He uttered a short scream.

The Farmer laughed and strolled back into the soggy, wooden building.

Louze patted the Nub's cheek. "That thing with the thumb was to let you know I'm serious about this. Some folk like to dink around, start with the little finger and work up—shit like that. Got too much respect for you. I can see you're serious about this. Serious as I am." Louze leaned back and grinned. "Desh, tell me every little thing about your friends, their army, and their plan of attack."

"I don't know any of that. I never saw the army. We rode ahead of them the whole time. That should be obvious!" The Nub scowled at Louze. "You're not really thinking this through, are you?"

Louze laughed and punched the Nub in the eye. "Damn, you don't mind talking it up tough, do you? Your answer makes sense, it does. You could be telling me the truth." Louze ran two steps forward, unleashed a thundering punch into the Nub's groin, and then slipped aside as the boy vomited.

The Nub moaned, "Why did you do that? I told you the truth!"

"Learn this quick, little friend. Sometimes I hurt you when you lie, and sometimes I hurt you when you say the truth. You'll never know which. Crazy, isn't it? The only way to stop the crazy is to tell me every damn thing you know. Don't hold back, and don't make me waste time asking. Then it'll stop."

Louze bent to pick through the items on the ground. He came up with a toy crossbow and a green triangular wooden block. "Tell me everything you think I might want to know. Even stuff you're not too sure about."

The Nub closed his eyes. Fingit heard the Nub mentally call him. "Fingit. Fingit. Fingit! Fingit!"

Fingit, unable to answer, glared at Sakaj.

"Fingit, you worthless bastard!" the Nub called out to Fingit in silence.

Louze chuckled. "Don't just hang there. I bet you haven't fainted or nothing. And you for sure aren't asleep. Tell me everything."

"I don't know anything!" he said to Louze.

"Well, that was sure as hell a lie." Louze paused. "Like I said, I won't hurt you at every lie. Let's talk about the leg. Son, I hear you can scoot right along, especially for a fellow minus a leg. Almost like you never were hurt. That peg leg of yours, which, pardon me, is uglier than the mole on my grandma's ass, has got to be magic. Tell me all about your leg."

The Nub craned his neck to look around. "Where is it?"

Louze grabbed the Nub's jaw hard. "Never you mind that. Answer."

"I made it," the Nub mumbled.

Louze pushed the Nub's face away. "Well, I figured that out already. But Lord Reth told me to ask you in particular, what did you trade for it?"

"Odd and ends." The Nub shrugged. "Nothing I'll miss."

"Uh-huh." Louze held up the two toys, moving them up and down as if they were on a scale. "Choose."

The Nub shook his head.

"I saw the blacksmith has a big goddamn pair of pliers a while ago. I could fetch them for us."

The Nub squirmed and silently called out, "Fingit! You come talk to me, you mangy horse's whang! I want to deal!"

Fingit looked away.

The Nub indicated the toy crossbow with his chin.

Louze dropped the block and held the crossbow up to the light. "Doesn't promise much. But the crosspiece is real iron and even a little sharp. Would you give such a thing to a child for him to play with? I'd think it was risky. Well, let's figure out something to do with it."

Sakaj said, "Don't worry, Fingit, we'll... find something."

Fingit hissed. *I can't believe I'm about to ask this, but shit, he's dead anyway.* "Sakaj, would you try to contact him?"

The Goddess of the Unknowable smiled. "I wondered when you would beg for my help. It's the logical solution." Sakaj closed her eyes and gazed up at the Nub through the window onto man. "Nub, heed me," she muttered. "Nub. Oh, Nub... I, a mighty god, call you. Nub! Nub, answer me!"

Fingit waved and turned away. "Give it up. The Veil must be blocking you."

"Bah! I almost got his attention. I could feel his mind! I'll try again."

"Don't bother. In my opinion as the greatest engineer in existence, you have no chance unless you already have a relationship with him. Like me. The one who can't talk to the hairy little stalk!"

Sakaj tried twice more to call the Nub to her. She brushed his mind at a level too deep for him to notice, but nothing more. "Oh, damn him, the inattentive little rodent! Damn him, damn Krak, and while we're damning things, damn you too!"

Over the next hour, Louze elicited answers from the Nub, often using the toy crossbow to inflict bruises, scrapes, and shallow cuts. The young man provided some bits of knowledge, but over-all, he resisted. Sakaj began deriding the man's torturing skills.

At that point, Louze used the tapered edge of the crosspiece to cut the skin between the Nub's thumb and forefinger. That proved a successful tactic, if the Nub's yelling and writhing meant anything. Louze then wandered away for a few minutes and returned with the previously mentioned pliers.

Fingit saw that Louze was now torturing in earnest. Of course, he wasn't surprised when Louze used the pliers to apply crushing force to the Nub's left nipple. That was almost compulsory in these types of affairs. Then Louze began sawing at the young man's chest with the iron crosspiece.

Sakaj raised her voice over the Nub's screams. "Is he attempting to cut the nipple off entirely?"

Fingit nodded. "I think he is. That shows a smidge of creativity. At least it does in my estimation."

"I won't be convinced until he accomplishes it. That's going to prove vexing with that marginally sharp bit of iron."

Two minutes later, Louze was still sawing away while holding the Nub's nipple in place with the pliers, even though everything was slippery with blood. The Nub howled and wept as he tried to twist away from the pain. Louze worked with a smile and showed no signs of fatigue.

A minute later, the Nub passed out. Louze kept at it until he had sawed the nipple off entirely. In the end, the task had required about five minutes, and it left the Nub dangling uncon-scious. As Louze washed his hands, he muttered, "Something ought to come out of that, eh? Shame I don't have days to do a full job on him before I kill him. Can't do everything you want, I guess. That's why they call it work."

Fingit stared at Sakaj, his mouth open. He allowed the world of mankind to fade from his hearing.

"Don't worry, I'll think of something!" Sakaj shouted, her

body quivering.

Fingit stood and stalked a few steps away. "You and your stupid rat-puking ideas!"

"Are you going to quit now, coward?"

"Oh, I don't know! When the Nub's dead, do you think we can fix this by dancing his corpse around like a puppet? Moron!"

Sakaj looked away, at least as far as she could with her entire body below the shoulders reduced to a gooey rug.

"What made you think that the Freak would deal?" Fingit shouted.

"She should have!" Sakaj shouted back. "Everything in her entire life, in her whole being, led up to that moment. There was no way she could have resisted."

"Well, I guess there was *some* way, wasn't there?" Fingit said in a singsong voice. "Now he's being tortured to death, and I'm going to lose the little meat chunk! He still has a lot of good trades in him!" Fingit sighed. "What are we going to do for power? What am I going to tell Krak?"

"Don't tell Krak anything! We can salvage this."

"Stop saying that! How in the nasty corners of the Void do you think we can we fix this?"

"I don't know yet, but I know we can. Trust me."

"Like I trusted you before? Like the Nub trusted me? Like anybody trusts anybody around here? Are you still insane? I trust you as far as I can piss whiskey!" Fingit's voice broke as he screamed at her.

Sakaj glared her disgust up at Fingit. "If I had feet, I would kick your balls through the top of your skull."

Fingit roared, "Well, I *do* have feet, and you're a pretty handy target, darling!"

"You wouldn't!"

Fingit ran toward Sakaj and aimed a kick directly at her nose. Unable to dodge or even flop out of the way, Sakaj closed her eyes.

Fingit exerted all his divine strength to pull the kick aside at the last moment, and it just caught her ear. Spinning, Fingit toppled to the grass.

Sakaj opened her eyes and released a trembling sigh. She whispered, "Thank you for not murdering me, at least.".

Fingit rose. "To hell with you." He grabbed her attenuated shoulders and lifted, and then he dragged her flattened body as if he were pulling a piece of lumber along by one end.

"Set me down!" Sakaj wiggled her body like a floppy rug as she repeated the command several times, accompanied by increasingly awful profanity.

Fingit dragged her down a gentle slope to a black pond. He hauled her into the knee-deep water and hurled her toward the middle, spinning like a fisherman's net. She smacked onto the surface, settled a moment, and sank.

Fingit waded out of the pond and trudged up the slope. Then he stopped and took a couple of uncertain steps back toward the pond. He looked around and saw that no one else seemed to be in Unicorn Town right then.

I really ought to fish her out. But she's probably not dead, and she can jump out of Unicorn Town whenever she wants. Of course, Krak will vaporize her once I tell him what's happened, so she might not be anxious to go home yet. And if she's dead forever? In that case, there's nothing I can do to help her anyway, is there?

Fingit turned away from the pond and began wandering through the Unicorn Town murk, thinking about how to explain this to the Father of the Gods so that Krak wouldn't vaporize him too.

THIRTEEN

(Sakaj)

S akaj concentrated on suppressing her anger. She found it difficult, especially with a black aquatic weed wafting up her nose. She told herself that if she had arms, she could fashion that weed into a strangling cord for the next time she saw Fingit. Or if she had a drop of power, she could come upon Fingit unaware, cast him into a magical sleep, and replace some of his intestines with the black weed. That shouldn't be impossible for the Goddess of the Unknowable.

But Sakaj did not have arms, so she may as well plan to carry Fingit off into the Void on a talking cow, there to destroy him beneath an avalanche of nasty hard cheeses. She considered it unlikely she could accomplish any of that, unless she now lay at the bottom of a mystical pond. She supposed that the pond could be mystical, considering that it existed in the Dark Lands. Yet unless it produced well-endowed love slaves, or a school of demon fish with which to destroy her enemies, it wasn't mystical enough to suit her.

All of my stratagems have failed. If we rely upon Harik and

Lutigan to fight our war, Cheg-Cheg will destroy us all. The Veil will never be lifted, and we'll die as demented, degenerate creatures. Well, to the hells with that! Krak certainly did not sire me on that chintzy tart he found out in the Void just for me to hand over my life uncontested. I heap filth upon capitulation! Instead, I shall conquer.

I wish this damned weed would get out of my nose.

Sakaj wiggled her nostrils to dislodge the aggravating strand of aquatic life. Amazingly, it worked.

Perhaps that's a good omen. Or perhaps I just have nostrils of godly might. Either way... the Freak is still the key. Perhaps it's still too hypothetical for her to care. I could present her with a greater pending disaster. Show her a few burned babies and disemboweled puppies. That would get her attention. Wouldn't it?

It gags me to even think it, but what if Fingit was correct? Was my plan too complicated? I could set the Freak aside for another time and work with that which is closer at hand. The Murderer has been mutilated. If I touch the Farmer, Harik will be bleating to Krak before I've drawn my third breath. That leaves the Nub, whom Fingit betrayed. Can I trick the Nub into calling on me?

The possibly mystical pool in which Sakaj lay measured just a few feet deep. She exerted all her divine powers of concentration, as well as her incipient panic, to perceive the window onto the world of man. After a long, grinding effort, she heard the voice of that ridiculous torturer. The torture hadn't yet reached its climax.

Louze was saying, "Talking about your leg, then, and your miraculous recovery—I can't nearly believe you are so tough, even using magic. Honestly, you haven't shown me much in the way of being tough-skinned. I don't want to hurt your feelings, of course." Louze whirled the crosspiece and smacked the Nub in the crotch. Even at the bottom of a pond on another world, Sakaj heard the young man groan. "You're not anything more than human, I don't think." He dragged the end of the crosspiece over the young man's intact nipple and murmured, "Hmm?"

After a pause, Louze sighed. "Well, to hell with that shit for now. Let's talk about military matters. What do you think? Would that be good?" The Nub's head drooped, and Louze slapped his face with the iron crosspiece. "How big is that army following along behind you? Is it dragging war engines? How many archers? How many whores? How much food and oil and arrows?"

Desh sighed and then spat blood, his head still drooping. "I don't know any of that."

Sakaj attempted to insinuate herself into the Nub's mind. It required astounding effort, particularly since she had to accomplish it unnoticed. It was like placing a flower on your lover's pillow without waking him, except that instead of gripping it in your delicate fingers, you must deposit it from the jaws of a slobbering hound that's strapped to your arm.

"Tell him," Sakaj mumbled to the Nub beneath his consciousness. "Tell him Sakaj's name."

The Nub hauled his face up toward his torturer. One eye was swelled shut, blood dripped from his mouth, and bruises stood in patchwork on the rest of his face. He hissed, "Fingit, Krak, and Sakaj will eat your rotting liver, Louze. They'll dangle your entrails for the dogs in hell."

"Fingit, Krak, and who?" Louze stepped back and stared at the Nub.

Only the near obliteration of all her limbs prevented Sakaj from dancing around like a deranged blowfly. The Nub had spoken the name of She-Who-Must-Not-Be-Named. It was an invitation for Sakaj to sweep into the world of man, claim everything she coveted, steal all the power she could transport, and destroy every other thing she wished to destroy.

Sakaj gathered her power and wrapped it inside the malice she bore for mankind and everything that might deny her glory—

especially Fingit. She held Louze and the Nub and the rotting building in her mind down to the tiniest detail. She willed herself into the world of man and then experienced a complete failure to shift herself even an inch out of that murky pond.

"No!" Sakaj shrieked. That was a mistake, and she swallowed a sizable quantity of nasty pond water. Rarely had she been called to the world of man, and this time the Veil had prevented her from answering.

Damn the Veil nine times nine! May it be swallowed by the unending chasms! May whoever created it... ah. Well, shit.

Louze leaned toward the Nub, and Sakaj strained to hear the man's whispers. "Ah, you poor little fellow. Your suffering has just about ended. But there's no mercy or hope for you today. Soon— maybe tonight or tomorrow or maybe in an hour—I'll come for you, and I will break, cut out, or tear away things you can never get back. You're going to tell me every secret, even the teeny tiniest. And when I've taken it all, then I'll set you free." He stepped back. "If you hadn't sneaked into Lord Reth's stronghold, I wouldn't have had to do all this horrible shit to you. Makes me a little sad for both of us."

Sakaj closed her eyes and tried to array all the players and variables against each other in various combinations. *Perhaps the Nub will liberate himself yet. I cannot see any way in which he might accomplish it, but I assume it's possible in some theoretical fashion. If he does, I must arrange matters so that he will call to me. With my subtle guidance, perhaps he will extricate himself. Then I shall suck the boy as dry as a beetle's husk before Fingit looks up from playing with his fingers. In the meantime, I should not like to return home just to be obliterated by Krak, yet Fingit will certainly bring Krak here soon anyway. I'll wait until I hear the hooting old loudmouth and then slip back home before he notices.*

(Fingit)

Fingit crashed through a low table built of rare pressed woods. Splinters scattered across Krak's music parlor floor. A black crystal vase shattered against the back of Fingit's head as he tumbled and smacked into the marble wall, just beneath a tasteful painting of Krak playing the harmonium. An iridescent rose from the vase came to rest on Fingit's throat. Five terrified burgundy and cobalt butterflies thrashed their way toward safety.

As he struggled to sit, Fingit touched the waterfall of blood now sliding toward the back of his collar.

That's not too bad. At least none of me is vaporized yet.

Krak seized the front of Fingit's shirt and hefted him into the air again. He tried to relax to lessen the likelihood of breaking a leg or skull when he got hurled again. Instead of throwing him, Krak yelled, "You squatty, ass-grabbing, idiotic, floppy-fluted, pipsqueak of a god! I should take you to Unicorn Town and tear you into a thousand pieces! Dumbass! You are eaten up with dumbass!"

Fingit felt pretty sure that no words ever uttered would make this situation any better for him, so he just gave a tiny smile. A line of blood trickled from the corner of his mouth, but he hoped the smile made him look contrite, anyway.

Krak heaved Fingit again, this time toward the middle of the room where no undestroyed obstacles remained. Fingit bounced against the marble floor, rolled, and skidded to a stop facedown. Krak put his hands on his hips. "You were the only one I trusted not to do something stupid. The Nub was our most reliable producer, and you threw him away!"

Fingit looked up. He tried to think of a different way to convince Krak this was all Sakaj's fault. He had attempted that when he first gave Krak the news. That was when Krak had started tossing him around like firewood. Therefore, Fingit jerked when Krak said, "Where's Sakaj?"

"I don't know for sure."

Krak walked across the room, kicking some scraps of furniture out of his way, and stood over Fingit. "Where did you last see her?"

"Unicorn Town."

"Come on." Krak yanked Fingit upright and pulled him through the expanding mansion to the room containing the now-permanent gallows. A minute later, they had hanged themselves; some unknown time after that, they awoke in Unicorn Town.

Krak squeezed Fingit's arm until it felt like it might pop in two. "Where was she?"

Unable to think of any reasonable explanations or delaying tactics, Fingit led Krak to the pond.

"Where, by the water?"

"No." Fingit pointed using the arm that wasn't being crushed. "Out there. Under the water."

"You drowned her?" Krak yelled.

"No!" Fingit pulled as far away as Krak's grip allowed. "Well, probably not."

Krak closed his eyes for a time, still holding Fingit. When he opened them, he said, "It grieved me when Fressa was killed and I lost one of my offspring in this war. It will grieve me twice as much if I've lost a second child in Sakaj." Krak squeezed harder, and Fingit felt watery shock that his arm wasn't crushed into powder. Krak showed Fingit his divinely brilliant teeth. "However, if you have caused me to lose that second child, I will not grieve at all to lose a third. Now, go get her if she's there."

Fingit waded to the spot where Sakaj had sunk, probed around for a bit, and even dove a couple of times. At last, he came up with Sakaj's clearly lifeless head, attached to her mostly flattened body.

I could go the other way. Just drop her and swim to the other side. Then all I'd have to do is elude Krak for the rest of eternity.

Fingit towed Sakaj's body to shore next to Krak. "She may not be dead. She may have just released her body on this side."

"We'll find out pretty soon. Until then, don't go anywhere without me."

"Fingit!" came the Nub's voice out of blackness.

Fingit gaped for a moment. Then he frowned at the sky until it swept and twisted to show the Nub. The young man had been tied and gagged with impressive skill. He had also been beaten and cut up with equally impressive skill. Fingit hadn't expected such thoroughness from that ape-armed human torturer. The Nub lay on his side, knees up, on a tall wooden bench inside a poorly torchlit building.

"The little ass-wart is alive," Krak grunted.

"There's still hope then!" Fingit smiled. He resisted the urge to jump around in supplication like some fluffy runt of a dog.

Krak stepped back and nodded. "Sure. There'd be more hope, of course, if you hadn't tricked him into the hands of his enemies and left him with no defense against being mutilated and murdered." Krak glared at his son. "That would have helped."

"Still..." Fingit gazed up at the Nub as if waiting for him to spontaneously pop out of his bonds.

Krak lay his hand on Fingit's shoulder with a meaty whack. "Fine, let's wait and observe the manner of his death. Do you want to make a game of it? Whatever the Nub's enemies do to him, I'll do to you?"

Fingit began a chuckle that turned into a cough when Krak didn't smile. He shook his head. Then he and Krak sat on the cushy black grass and listened to the Nub call Fingit a dozen more times in the next hour. Fingit sagged more with each call that he couldn't answer. After the fourth pleading look that he tossed at Krak, the Father of the Gods waved Fingit away. "There's no point in my calling out to him. I can't reach out to him through the Veil, and I doubt he'll call me."

"I know." Fingit sagged.

"Then stop slumping and sighing. It's ungodlike."

The Nub called Fingit seven more times. Then the young man called in a shaky voice, "Krak?"

Krak jerked. "Might as well. I can't make things any more awful than you've already made them, eh?"

Fingit jumped up. "Wait! He has to save himself, but since you can't just say, 'We can't help you,' could you, oh, somehow imply a little bit that he can save himself if he really tries?"

Krak looked at Fingit as if he were a backward sheep. "That's almost the same as helping him. Do you want me to give him a magic sword and make him impervious too?"

"I know, you're right, but maybe you could get the idea across. Indirectly."

Krak rubbed his gigantic jaw. "Maybe I could—if I combine subtlety with cruel indifference."

"You are just the god for that." Fingit gazed upon Krak with such overwhelming hero worship that even a child could see it was false.

Krak snorted, and he even grinned a little. "You little shit." Krak drew the Nub closer, and the sorcerer appeared from out of the blackness. "What do you want?" Krak thundered. "How dare you interrupt me! I am the damned Father of the Gods! Who the hell are you?"

"I'm sorry." The Nub cringed. "I'll go now."

"Hell, you're here already. You might as well say what you want."

"I've been tortured and am being held prisoner, Father Krak."

"You're boring me. I don't want to know what happened to you yesterday. What do you want right now?"

"I want to escape." The Nub emphasized that with a clenched fist.

"Go ahead and do that."

The Nub deflated a bit. "I want your help to escape."

Krak answered in a tight voice, just above a whisper. "Hold it right there! What do you think is going on here? Do you expect the gods to jump down from our mighty thrones to untie knots for you or put out fires that you started? Be honest. That doesn't sound very logical, does it?"

"No, it doesn't." The Nub seemed to shrink further.

"Now," Krak said as if they were speaking over the dinner table, "look at your current situation, which is being held prisoner, right? How did they bind you? A cell? Chains? Suspended from a cliff and being pecked by ravens? What?"

"I'm tied up."

"What, with rope?" Krak smirked at Fingit.

"Um..."

"Rope!" Krak shouted. "You called on the gods because of a little dead grass? Every sorcerer in history would puke if they knew that." Despite their impending decline and destruction, Krak and Fingit gritted their teeth and covered their mouths to keep from giggling aloud.

The Nub said, "I'm sorry. I guess I'm a poor sorcerer, but I don't know how to untie myself."

"By the Black Whores and their black hearts! Sorcerer, assuming you have enough imagination to fill a gnat's ear, list seven ways to get out of rope bonds."

"Well, untying them. Cutting, burning, and breaking. Getting somebody else to untie them. Chewing through them. Tricking an animal into chewing through them..."

Krak grunted. "That's enough. Now, if you keep on thinking, I'm sure you'll come up with a way to free yourself—without bothering the most powerful being in all existence!"

"Yes, Father Krak."

"Don't bother me anymore. Not for at least a week, anyway." Krak hurled the Nub away in just the same manner he'd hurled Fingit all over the music parlor.

Krak leaned back and watched the Nub struggle in his bonds. "Maybe that will do it. It would have been better if I could have just traded with him, of course. Even if I destroyed him in the process, I might have gotten enough power to save us."

"Maybe he'll save himself, and we'll get another chance."

Krak shrugged. "Maybe Cheg-Cheg will die from a disease of the penis, and I'll build a summer cottage in his skull."

FOURTEEN

(Sakaj)

"Will you please cease fiddling with that collar and put your head through the noose?" With one hand on her hip, Sakaj successfully implied that her words were a request, a command, and an insult woven together.

Harik slurred as he answered. "I still find it incomprehensible that Krak requires our presence with such urgency, since your 'window onto man' has to date demonstrated an absolute lack of worth and shows no promise of providing value in the future. How does he get this thing to lay flat?" Harik writhed, trying to adjust Krak's favorite coat into a better position on his shoulders, and he once again smoothed the fur collar. It was made from the surpassingly fluffy tail-tufts of infant manticores. Harik had complimented his father on the coat many times, and he had giggled upon finding it unattended. However, when Harik filched the coat to admire himself in it, he found that the Father of the Gods possessed a mighty frame with a chest of mythical dimensions, and Harik's merely godlike chest seemed sickly in comparison. Thus, the collar wrinkled.

"Take that off, you idiot." Lutigan swayed as he yanked his own noose down around his neck. "You look like a mouse wearing a steel pot. Besides, there's no one in the Dark Lands for you to impress into rutting with you."

One of Krak's mostly unclothed demigoddess servants was holding a mirror in which Harik could admire himself. The God of Death winked at her. She smiled and winked back.

"You two proceed without me," Harik said. "I suspect this is nothing of consequence really, just some trifle Krak may have mentioned and that Sakaj misapprehended to a stupendous degree. If it does amount to something, return and fetch me."

Sakaj stepped between Harik and the tarty servant. "I don't think I could have misunderstood the words 'most profound crisis since the beginning of time.' I also doubt that I misheard 'bring Harik and Lutigan, or everyone will be destroyed forever.' Those are simple and unambiguous statements, if you ask me."

Harik frowned and fluffed the collar once more.

Sakaj launched a vehement sigh his direction. *I just wanted to bring these fools back to the Dark Lands so Krak might not kill me right away. Two more stupid gods bumbling around ought to confuse matters. And if necessary, I'll think of a way to sacrifice one of them.*

But the two inebriated gods hadn't wanted to go. The Dark Lands were boring, except for the horrifying parts in which Cheg-Cheg tried to kill them. Krak's mansion contained plenty of liquor, food, and balconies with warm breezes. It also contained a staff of lovely servants ready for some cheerful frolicking on one of the plush couches or divans. Lutigan and Harik had explained with great emphasis how much they did not want to go to the Dark Lands.

Sakaj's mistake had been telling these sated and recumbent gods, "Krak commands our presence in the Dark Lands." It was a lie of course, but it should have been easy to believe. Yet they had refused to go, and each of their subsequent refusals forced Sakaj to restate Krak's supposed command with more emphasis and less relation to the truth. Her final effort included limitless wine and love slaves for everyone who obeyed Krak. Also, those who disobeyed could expect to be chained to a stone and eviscerated every day for a thousand years, with their entrails arranged to spell out profane verses belittling their sexual prowess.

That had finally gotten them moving. Sakaj hoped they were too drunk to remember any of this. "Harik! If you don't come with us, I'll tell Krak that you called him too impotent and stupid to be obeyed. And I'll tell him you're putting your nasty hands all over his things."

Harik hissed an oath so monumental that Sakaj blushed, but he slipped the noose over his head and shrugged out of the voluminous coat. "Perhaps you should hold in mind that I am capable of prevaricating to your detriment, should you choose to—"

Lutigan kicked Harik in the shin. As the God of Death yelped and leaned forward, Sakaj shoved him off his chair. After a short interval of kicking, spitting, and drooling, Harik, in his inert form, suspended from the beam.

"I'd trade him for a crooked spear and then burn the spear." Lutigan grunted. Then he jumped off his chair, followed by Sakaj half a breath later.

Sakaj had gained more experience with the Dark Lands than any other god, and perhaps more than any other being in existence. She possessed a crude ability to arrive there a modest distance away from the common entry point. As she swung and kicked toward elevation, she shifted her desired entry as far from that common point as possible, which should also be as far from an enraged and murderous Krak as possible. At the last moment, she convulsed with panic, realizing that she might have unthinkingly placed herself in that damned, not-so-mystical pond again. Then she elevated.

When Sakaj awoke in the Dark Lands, she drew air into her lungs rather than water. That was a relief, and she used that air to express her relief with half a sigh. The second half was cut off and trapped inside her by a ponderous force descending on her throat. She looked up, writhed, and grabbed at the all-powerful, sandal-shod foot of her father as it pressed her neck into the dark grass. None of that helped her, so she offered a gesture of inoffensive submission and just accepted whatever Krak wanted to do to her.

Krak bent, wound his great, rootlike fingers into Sakaj's hair, and dragged her upright while she gagged. "You've completed my happiness, daughter. You live, and now you can sit at my knee as we watch all our hopes fail because of you and that nitwit Fingit. We could also toast to our grisly extinction if only we had a single damned thing to drink in this place." Krak lifted her to his full height with the deliberation of a glacier and then shook her. She felt hairs popping free of her scalp. "Thank you, my daughter. Thank you for being such a selfish, petty, arrogant little scut of a god. You've done a phenomenal job of destroying us. We can now celebrate the dregs of our glory."

Sakaj tried to glance around, but she couldn't see past Krak's monumental shoulders and head. With a shadowy grin, she said, "If I'd known we were celebrating, I would have worn a nicer dress." Maybe those would be her last words, but they sounded better than, "Please, please don't kill me."

Krak dropped her, and she clambered upright, hand pressed to the half-bald patch on her scalp. She saw Fingit standing just behind Krak's shoulder, like a good little sycophant. Harik and Lutigan stood farther back. Lutigan's shoulders were sagging, and Harik's eyes appeared terrified and were full of tears.

Krak looked at the sky, and Sakaj joined in as everyone else looked too. She scanned the scene. *Let's see, this is some sort of run-down wooden building lit by a torch or two. It's nighttime. The Nub's tied and gagged on that bench, and that man looks to be guarding him. There's the Farmer talking with his hooligan and ignoring the Nub. Well... damn it to my mother's heart.*

Then Sakaj jerked upright. "Maybe there's time! I can call the Freak!" Without waiting for anyone to agree, disagree, or throw a shoe at her, Sakaj sent the image swirling and shot it across the landscape to find the Freak. Everybody stared at her as she spoke up through the window onto mankind. "Daughter. My daughter, heed me. Your mother calls—come to her. Now. Don't make me wait. Young lady, you come here right now!" The Freak continued creeping through a narrow, wet cave, and she didn't acknowledge Sakaj's call in any way.

Fingit punched her on the arm. "Give up. I expect she's shutting you out without even knowing it. If only you were strong like in the old days, huh? Then she couldn't ignore you." He shrugged and gave her a dry smile.

Sakaj glowered over at Harik and scrambled for something to say that would dissuade him from bargaining with the Farmer and stealing Sakaj's glory. Harik shrugged at her. "I already have a significant active bargain in progress with the Farmer. I attempted to strike others with him, but he has refused."

Krak grabbed Sakaj's arm. "Don't drift away. I want you right beside me to watch all this." Krak swung the image back to the Nub.

The Farmer and his hanger-on strode out the building. On the way out, the Farmer nodded to the soldier guarding the Nub. The man looked around, sat down on a wobbling chair, and held his sword across his knees while he watched the Nub breathe.

Lutigan said, "I hope the little shit-eater is smart, because he sure doesn't look tough."

The gods settled on the grass. Fingit and Harik started arguing about whether existence could continue once Cheg-Cheg had murdered all the gods. Over the next few minutes, they concluded that the monster was really just destroying himself and he'd go away if only somebody could make him understand that. Krak commanded them to go right out and explain it all to Cheg-Cheg. Or, if they'd rather, they could shut the hell up and let Krak enjoy the end of existence in peace.

Sakaj didn't look away from the Nub. Before long, he smacked the bench with the heel of his remaining foot.

The soldier spit on the wooden floor covered in sloppy grime. "What?"

Still gagged, the Nub pushed up with one elbow until he sat on the edge of the bench. He bent forward and strained as if he were passing a crocodile egg.

"Hold on to it," the soldier said.

The Nub strained again, producing a spectacular five-second fart that spanned an octave and a half.

"Gah! What did you eat, a demon's balls? Fine, come on. Stay in front."

The Nub hopped on his one leg to the door. The soldier pointed left and gave a little push, knocking the Nub flat on the grass. The solider helped him stand, but on the one-minute hop to the latrine, the Nub fell twice more.

At the latrine, the Nub held up his bound hands.

The soldier leaned against the wall. "Forget it."

The Nub raised his eyebrows and shrugged at the soldier.

"Hell no, I'm not wiping your ass! Just shit and get moving."

The Nub looked at his belt and then back up at the soldier.

"Fine! Face the wall." The soldier lowered the Nub's trousers.

The Nub relieved himself, was reclothed, and hopped back to the wooden building, where he flopped onto the bench.

"Our hopes rest with this boy?" Harik dropped his face into one hand. "We deserve to be extinguished."

Lutigan sneered. "I may never have seen a more disappointing performance by a sorcerer."

Krak held up a hand. "Hush. You're acting ungodly. Of all the times one should be dignified, death is the most important of all."

"What bullshit!" Sakaj overheard Lutigan whisper to Harik, but Krak didn't react.

"I wish we had something to drink." Fingit sat up. "I can bring drinks here from the other side—"

"Stay here." Krak dropped his hand like a felled tree onto Fingit's shoulder.

Sakaj lay back and put her hands behind her head. She examined the little stick that the Nub had picked up on one of his falls. *None of them saw it. How long will it take them?*

The Nub had turned his back to the guard, his hands worrying with the stick. It wasn't much longer than his palm, and Sakaj saw nothing unusual about it. It wasn't even straight. The boy gripped it with his left fingers only since his broken thumb stuck out useless. He scraped at the stick with his right thumbnail and fingernails.

About a minute later, the Nub started sawing at the ropes with the little stick. The ropes began fraying.

Sakaj stood. "Perhaps we should recruit the Nub to lead our armies against Cheg-Cheg. He did not merely fool his guard. He fooled all of you."

Before the exclamations, insults, and expressions of insecurity died away, the Nub cut through the rope that was binding his hands.

Lutigan raised his voice over everyone else. "Don't get excited. He has one leg, two free hands, and a tiny stick. He's a pissant baby sorcerer."

The Nub rolled off the bench and flopped onto the floor like a ham. Before the gods could express dismay, the Nub reached out and jabbed the top of the soldier's foot with the end of the stick. The thing must have been pointy as well as sharp on the edge, because the soldier yelped and bent over. The Nub grabbed the soldier's collar with the fingers of his left hand, stabbed him beneath the ear, and dragged the stick halfway around the man's neck. As blood sprayed from the neck wound, the soldier fell backward in his chair, over, and onto the floor. He gasped, writhed, and bled.

"Yes!" Fingit stood and clapped his hands toward the sorcerer's image. "Listen to me, Nub! Nub!"

Krak grinned. "You'd better get to bargaining with him before someone puts a sword through the little cripple's head."

All of the gods shouted and gave advice, but the Nub did not call. He used the soldier's sword to pull himself upright, and then he hopped to the door again.

"Nub! Listen to me! Listen!" Fingit shouted.

The Nub didn't appear to have heard Fingit at all.

The Nub won't call Fingit. He won't even answer the grimy dwarf. He thinks Fingit has deserted him. Sakaj punched Fingit on the arm. "Not like the old days, eh?"

Fingit swore and then walked off a little distance to pout.

"He needs to get moving!" Lutigan growled.

Sakaj saw Louze, the torturer, ambling back to the rotting house. He would spot the Nub in less than a minute. The Nub turned right and hopped toward the scaffold, the toy-strewn grass, and the woodpile that held his leg. He tripped and fell under the scaffold, and the sword flew out of his hand into the darkness. He sat up, looked toward Louze, and froze.

"Call me now!" Fingit shouted.

The Nub whispered, "Harik!"

"No! The Void suck it to eternity!" Fingit screamed, aiming a kick at the God of Death.

Harik sidestepped and stumbled a little. He slurred a bit when he said, "The young man knows what he wants."

Sakaj bared her teeth. *Oh, Harik's going to do it. That nasty, mincing, porcelain god is going to set all this right and be the hero, and I'll be the runt piglet for the rest of time. I should kill Harik instead. One insane blow. He won't have a chance to leave his body before he's dead.*

May the Void drown me in shit. I'm not going to let this happen. I don't care if we all die.

Sakaj leaped two steps toward Harik and kicked his feet from under him. His back hit the grass, and he stared up at her with his stupid, fish-eyed expression. She didn't hesitate before hurling herself down at him, the point of her elbow aimed at the center of his face. Krak and Fingit were yelling, and Lutigan brushed her shoulder as he grabbed for her. She landed with all her weight on Harik's nose, smashing it with a crunching sound that provided her enormous satisfaction. His nose penetrated his brain, and the God of Death's eyes went blank in an instant.

Now everyone was shouting. As Krak stalked toward her, Sakaj rolled to her knees and said, "A shame about Harik. He won't be collecting from the Nub now, though."

Everyone stopped, and Sakaj stood. "However, the Nub knows my name. I predict he'll call on me. So, unless you want to scratch at dirt, grunt, and pass waste from your butt like humans for an eon or two—at best—I'm the only chance you have left."

FIFTEEN

(Sakaj)

Harik's dead, smashed face stared up into the window on man. He looked as if he were still longing for the power—and the license to gloat that he'd almost won. Without the Nub's power, the gods might still have a small chance to escape annihilation, only to fall into degradation.

Sakaj gazed at the corpse's face from one foot away. *That slop-pool was far more concerned about gloating than about saving the gods.*

Lutigan sighed. "I never liked Harik, but he was family. Maybe the rutting dog jumped away in time. But he was surprised, and he was drunk, and he never was all that bright."

Fingit squinted at Sakaj, who still crouched over Harik's body like a panther, feral and regal. He whispered, "Maybe the Veil didn't make her crazy. Maybe she's crazy all on her own."

Sakaj turned and grinned at him.

Every god had elevated every other god thousands of times, except for Krak, who had never been elevated by one of his children. They had murdered out of anger, frustration, or just because there wasn't anything else fun to do. The victim always returned the next day, in all his divine perfection, so it hadn't mattered that much. The Dark Lands had introduced them to death everlasting.

Krak stomped toward Sakaj, who could almost feel the ground trembling. She stood, and he stopped chest-to-face with her, overwhelming her slight form with his imponderable presence.

She set her shoulders back and smiled at him.

Krak spoke with the sound of mountains being crushed. "Betrayer, you have slain your brother and snatched your chance. So make it good. Do you need power to trade?"

Sakaj stepped away from Krak and shook her head. "I hid the power that Fingit gave me when he first swindled the Nub. Back when he was in love with me." She blew a kiss at Fingit and looked back up at the Nub, who still crouched in the darkness.

"Harik! Harik!" the Nub called to the gods. "Where are you? Are all the gods at some festival? Who takes care of existence while they're drunk and screwing around?" The Nub giggled with a touch of hysteria. "Harik?"

Louze had come within a hundred feet of the Nub when the sorcerer silently called, "Sakaj?"

Sakaj answered, "Yes, mighty sorcerer, I hear you."

Fingit looked away.

Sakaj smiled at Fingit's back. *I suppose he'd almost rather be expunged from the universe than watch me appropriate his sorcerer.*

The Nub appeared from darkness. "What's wrong?"

"How do you mean, Nub?" Sakaj asked.

"You called me mighty sorcerer, even though I'm squatting here all beaten up with things cut off me and filth on my ass. I'm as vain as any other sorcerer, but I'm not pure-bone stupid. So, what's wrong?"

"Are you quite certain you wish to speak to the Goddess of the Unknowable in that way?"

The Nub shrugged. "Oh, I apologize for saying that. I also want to say that your approach is as clumsy as it is obvious. I could call you a sickly cow too, but that would be rude."

"Aren't you charming?" Sakaj flung the Nub back into the world of man.

Fingit grabbed at the sleeve of Sakaj's blue gown. "Bring him back and let me talk to him!"

The Nub silently said, "Whenever you're ready, Sakaj. I don't hold a grudge."

Louze walked another twenty feet closer to the Nub, who silently said, "Fine, Sakaj. I'll take him with my little stick-knife. Watch me."

Sakaj uttered a lengthy, complex curse involving the Void, the Five Demon Cows of the Fissures, three bodily functions, two intimate parts of Krak's body, and a cactus. Then she pulled the Nub up to trade. "You know very well that torturer will spill your intestines and fertilize a garden on that spot with them."

"Maybe. I won't trade just anything to you, even for my life." The Nub crossed his arms.

"So you say before you're under his blade, Nub."

Krak whispered, "Just trade something with the little peach pit, already!"

"So you say, mighty Sakaj. I think we understand one another better."

Sakaj sneered and let it fill her voice. "Oh, you may be sure that we do." *The Nub doesn't understand anything about anything. Perhaps I can squeeze him dry of everything he values. I'll ruin him for Fingit!*

"I want power." The Nub said it as if he were asking for a clean mug. "Five squares should be enough. Please make an offer."

Sakaj took a breath, calmed herself, and made her voice as languid as a serpent. "Since I have already anticipated everything you could possibly say to me, I have an offer at hand. For five squares, you shall father a child and then leave it at the crossroads nearest its birthplace."

"I guess you intended that to sound poetic, mighty Sakaj, but no. I'll build a monument to you. A small one, no bigger than a donkey." The Nub held up his hand at just the height of a donkey.

"Pathetic. For four squares, you will father a child. Once it walks, it shall be cursed to kill its weight in creatures or men every day until it dies."

The Nub dared to laugh. "Definitely no. I'll tattoo 'She-Who-Must-Not-Be-Named' on my chest. For four squares."

Ooh. What manner of curses might I visit upon him through the agency of that tattoo? But it is not enough power for our purposes. "While that is flattering in a slutty way, no. Let us bring the bargain to three squares, and whenever you create something, you must destroy something equally precious."

The Nub laughed again, louder, and then paused. "For three squares, I won't be able to laugh for a month."

"A meager offer. For three squares, you shall never know happiness."

"Forget it. I won't laugh for a year. Three squares."

"No, that is not enough."

"What do you mean, mighty Sakaj?" The Nub peered around. "Do you need a certain type of sacrifice for something? What do you need?"

"You idiotic lump!" Krak whispered. "Why did you give him that bit of information? Has deicide clouded your thinking?"

Sakaj shook her head. *The Nub is just a young man, almost a baby. He doesn't know what he knows.* "It was a figure of speech. I was merely commenting on the deficiency of your offer. You will not know happiness for ten years in exchange for three squares."

"So that's the amount you need. Well, I might consider it then. But not for three squares."

"Four squares then, but you're stretching my patience like a harp string. If I let you die now, it wouldn't diminish my joy at this evening's dance."

"Good lie," Lutigan whispered. "That was convincing."

"I want an open-ended debt." The Nub yawned. "Five squares every day, forever."

Even though the end of all things was at hand, the gods all laughed in silence.

Sakaj kicked at the black grass. "Perhaps you would like a goldfish that grants wishes too? Hm? No! Of course not! No god has ever paid an open-ended debt, and I will not be the first! Take five squares or accept death."

"No, Sakaj. I can hear that you need this. Three squares per day, open-ended."

"Bah! Bah, fie, and ram your offer up your pinched human ass!"

The Nub said, "Oh, you really do need this, don't you?"

An earthquake thundered and crashed into existence on the other side of the pond in the Dark Lands. Sakaj looked around and saw Cheg-Cheg's head emerging from the ground.

"No, I don't!" Sakaj's voice implied that yes, she might. "You... just go off to die if you want to! Or you can take six squares and be denied happiness for ten years."

"Two squares per day, forever."

Krak whispered, "Do not take an open-ended debt, Sakaj. Better that we all die. It would be an appalling precedent. Every being in the Void would mock us."

Cheg-Cheg had climbed fully out of the ground, shaking Dark Lands dirt off like he was a dog. He pointed at the gods and roared.

The whole Void can suck itself out of existence for all I care! "No! No, no, no! Seven squares!" Sakaj screamed.

"Two squares per day, forever. Otherwise, I'm taking my

chances with Louze back there." The Nub pointed in a random direction, since he couldn't see Louze at all.

Cheg-Cheg charged across the pond, rather agile for a creature with the same mass as a hill.

Krak bellowed, "You will not make this bargain!"

"Father Krak?" the Nub said.

All the gods but Sakaj dropped to the ground as they abandoned their bodies.

"Just a few seconds more..." Sakaj knelt as she watched Cheg-Cheg knock down ancient trees like they were toddlers. "You will not know happiness for twenty years, in exchange for... one square per day. Open-ended. Forever."

"The power to accumulate every day!" the Nub said.

"No! All right! Yes! Done!"

Sakaj tossed today's power to the Nub. "Such a pleasure being utterly violated by you! Bastard!"

The Nub nodded as if he'd just purchased a pair of boots. "I'll call on you again some time."

An avalanche of power enveloped Sakaj.

The sorcerer snatched the wooden toy porpoise off the ground and held it between his knees. He began scratching a symbol on it with the iron crosspiece that Louze had used to saw off his nipple.

As Cheg-Cheg's impossible nightmare of a hand swept toward her, Sakaj abandoned her body in the Dark Lands.

SIXTEEN

(Fingit)

Fingit's new armor pinched a little in the crotch, but he'd forged it in a rush. Considering that he had created armor and weapons of divine power for twelve gods, and that he'd accomplished it before Cheg-Cheg had shown up to squash his new forge flatter than Weldt's penises, anyone who wanted to quibble about the tailoring could just bite themselves on the ass.

Sakaj had provided the power required for all of this.

Amazing how all was forgiven when she showed up with a positive ocean of power. Krak even hugged her.

Now that the gods were preparing for battle, Sakaj handed out power as if it were sand. Fingit had asked her, "Why so generous? You wanted that power so much you killed Harik like he was vermin. *Almost* killed." Harik had abandoned his body at the last instant and survived.

Sakaj clenched a fist between her breasts. "All victory now flows through me."

Fingit waited for more. When it didn't come, he said, "Good to know. I'll engrave that on the buttocks of your armor."

Krak used some of Sakaj's power to remove the taint of insanity from the land so all the gods could fight Cheg-Cheg in their homeland. Chira, Goddess of Forests, prepared the ground for battle. Lutigan called his fourteen demigod shield-men, although his host of fourteen thousand warriors had withered to fourteen thousand fat, old, or dead men. Harik and his wife, Trutch, the Goddess of Life, fueled their battle-rage by arguing about what Harik had been doing while she had been trapped in dirt-eating insanity.

Fingit's labor had delivered to each god the finest example of his or her preferred weapon. Lutigan's two fourteen-palms-length swords could cleave iron or granite. Harik's javelins delivered lightning, Chira's bow never missed, and Casserak's spear shook the earth like an avalanche. Sakaj might find it difficult to strike the decisive blow against Cheg-Cheg using her strangling cord, but that wouldn't be Fingit's fault. He'd made the thing deceptively strong and long.

Madimal, God of Deep Waters, came to Fingit to talk about his weapon. "Fingit, you pathetic squint, what the barking hell is this? A net?"

Fingit looked at the net in Madimal's hand and then pointed at it. "You traditionally fight with a net."

"That's when I'm fighting regular Void-beasts, or Lutigan's flunkies. What am I going to do, capture Cheg-Cheg's little finger?"

"Give it here."

Fingit led Madimal out behind the Forge of Thunder and Woe. "See that tree? The big one on the left? Well, screw that tree." Fingit hurled the net, and in midair, it stretched out large enough to cover not only the tree but also the entire hillside. "It gets big enough to grab whatever you want it to grab, up to a certain point. That certain point is about as big as a hillside."

Madimal still looked skeptical. "Fair enough. But what do I do then? Drag Cheg-Cheg to the ground like a runaway pig?"

"Say the magic words. Go on."

"Bite my ass!"

The entire net erupted in flames too brilliant to look at. When they had faded, nothing larger than a blackened stump stood on the hillside—apart from the undamaged net.

Fingit said, "The magic words to retrieve the net are, 'Fingit is a genius.'" The net refolded as it returned to him, and he handed it back to Madimal.

"I guess it will do." The God of Deep Waters trudged away.

Fingit hefted his new hammer, the Mallet of Indefensible Devastation. It could crush any object or creature that was hard. The harder it was, the better his hammer could crush it. At least, that's what Fingit had forged it to do. He wasn't 100 percent confident he'd succeeded. Nor was he entirely sure the other gods' weapons could do just exactly what he'd promised. It was a bit of a rush job, but everything should work out fine. He was 99 percent sure.

However, the gods' new armor provided unparalleled protection, if not comfort. Fingit felt unbending conviction about that. He admitted he might have spent a bit more time on his own armor than on the others' armor. In fact, he'd spent more time on his armor than on all the other armor put together. But no one could fault him for concern about his own survival. At least, they couldn't if they didn't know.

Ever since the first time Cheg-Cheg had bellowed and stomped around their land, the gods had always driven the Void-beast away by fighting it—and hurting it—within the Home of the Gods. Krak therefore planned to fight Cheg-Cheg in the Gods' Realm today. At dawn, he arrayed his forces for battle. However, by midday, Cheg-Cheg had not arrived.

"Think Cheg-Cheg's taking the day off?" Fingit scanned the

horizon with his Spyglass That Sees through Things That Aren't Too Thick.The name was pathetic, but Fingit had named it in disgust when he found it couldn't see through thick things.

Krak, transcendent and exalted in his white armor that was one-eighth as bright as sunlight, grimaced down at Fingit from where they both stood at the summit of Mount Humility. "Shut up. I'm the Father of the Gods, so I don't get cold, but my testicles are like raisins. No more talk about Cheg-Cheg not coming."

Fingit glanced at Sakaj, who stood at Krak's other hand, shimmering in her armor of several colors—the Suit of Ambiguous Mischance. She raised an eyebrow at Fingit as if he were a dog that had trotted face-first into a glass door.

Krak was keeping Fingit and Sakaj with him for the battle. Fingit had felt honored, until Krak said it was because he didn't trust them worth a damn. The other gods were scattered in the valleys beneath Krak's vantage.

Fingit had crafted each god's armor in his or her accustomed color. Sparkly-blue Gorlana, iron-gray Weldt, and his wife, passion-red Effla, were hiding on the right. Blood-red Lutigan and his drab thugs hid on the left, along with void-black Harik. The remaining four hid behind Lutigan. Flashing-yellow Trutch, holly-green Chira, deep ocean-blue Madimal, and ale-brown Casserak completed the wicked pantheon. From the top of Mount Humility, they looked like gaudy berries, some of which must be poisonous. Fingit grinned down at them and shifted against the pinch in the crotch of his steel armor that he had polished as bright as a mirror. He hoped they were all staying alert down there. Even at their best, most of the gods didn't have much of an attention span.

Later in the afternoon, just when Fingit was thinking about saying some other stupid thing, Cheg-Cheg's full, volcano-like roar reached them. Fingit inspected the horizon, but Cheg-Cheg must have been too far away for even a god's eyes to perceive him.

Krak grunted and raised a golden horn half again as long as he was tall. He sounded a vibrating blast, almost too low to be heard. The pathetic, whip-thin vegetation in front of him quivered and then collapsed.

Cheg-Cheg roared again. He roared three more times in the next two minutes, and each time, he sounded closer. Within another minute, the titanic creature rushed into view, approaching the gods at a relaxed lope.

Krak released the impossibly searing light of the sun, which crackled across the valley and struck distant Cheg-Cheg on his broad, feathery purple forehead. The beast twitched but didn't stop. The only damage Fingit could see was a few smoking feathers. Cheg-Cheg doubled his pace and ran straight toward Krak.

Krak bellowed laughter like a god. "That was just to get his attention!"

Fingit nodded. He was too nervous to make even a bad joke.

Cheg-Cheg reached the foothills a few thousand feet beneath Krak. The monster slowed, looked around, and ripped a gigantic pine tree out of the ground. Before he could hurl the tree, Weldt jumped out from hiding near the monster, whirled his sling, and shot a flaming lead ball into Cheg-Cheg's armpit. The foul, monstrous armpit hair began smoldering.

As Cheg-Cheg flapped his arm to stifle the fire, Effla sprinted past Weldt, a bright-red slash brandishing a sword quite a bit taller than her. Fingit smiled because he could hear the sword singing from where he stood. The singing sword would drain the monster's will if she could pierce its skin. Or maybe the beast would just feel faint. Or maybe nothing would happen. But the singing itself was a nice effect, anyway. Effla leaped the last ten paces to Cheg-Cheg's leg and swung at the black, leathery shin with all her godly power. The sword bounced off with a discordant note, and she bounced with it, right into Gorlana. The two of them tumbled another hundred feet before rolling to a stop.

Effla's failed attack hadn't even gotten the monster's attention. With one arm pressed down tight to smother the armpit blaze, the monster flung the pine tree at an improbable velocity, even for a huge supernatural being. The tree trunk landed on Weldt with a gargantuan explosion of dirt clods around the supine, iron-gray deity. Fingit told himself that since Weldt was protected by magical armor, he should be able to survive even that attack. Cheg-Cheg snatched the tree like a switch and smashed Weldt five more times. As the god's decapitated head sailed into a stand of timber, the great Void-beast tossed the tree over his shoulder a quarter mile up the mountainside. Fingit didn't lie to himself about Weldt surviving that. The elevated god should be on his way to the Dim Lands right then.

Cheg-Cheg began climbing the mountain. A rainbow of six more gods plus Lutigan's fourteen nasty thugs assaulted the monster from behind. This was the main attack. The demigods charged all around to confuse the monster. Lutigan hacked at the Void-beast's Achilles tendon, leaving shallow cuts that released a foul vapor like hissing steam. Harik threw lightning-javelins at Cheg-Cheg's gibbous, yellow eyes, and Chira shot arrows up his pug nose. Casserak thrust her spear under one of the creature's luminous, white talons to stab the nail bed. Trutch leaped atop the beast's immense foot like an insane, yolk-dipped shrew. She flailed with her ax, with a zero probability of hurting him at all.

Madimal hurled his net, and it spun out to an enormous diameter suitable for enveloping Cheg-Cheg. The monster stuck out one horrifying finger, snagged the net, and collected the collapsing net into one hand. He chucked it back toward the river valley, and it disappeared past the horizon. It might have sailed past the valley, or out of the Gods' Realm entirely.

"Now!" Krak bellowed. He ran down the mountainside to join the fight, a boulder of incandescence gaining speed. Fingit and Sakaj followed him.

Cheg-Cheg stiffened and turned under the coordinated attack, looking back the way he had come. Then he staggered three steps backward away from the mountain.

"He's going to run!" Fingit shouted. "He's breaking!"

Indeed, Cheg-Cheg took another step back and lowered his head, streamers of acid-drool pouring down to dissolve the foliage and soil. Then the monster sighed and shook his head, reminding Fingit of a frazzled mother who had found filth tracked onto her clean floor. Fingit stopped shouting about victory. He ran faster instead.

The monster roared. Every raucous noise the gods had heard from the monster throughout history was immediately reclassified. Many were relegated to "bellow" status, and a good number were recognized to be "howls." Very few became "yawps." The measure of a Cheg-Cheg roar became how far it tumbled you across the landscape, and how much blood gushed from your ears, nose, and eyes.

Fingit tumbled "pretty far" and gushed "a lot." The roar had hurled him almost back to the foothills by the time he stopped himself. Everyone else was dragging and staggering to their feet, including Lutigan's demigods. Fingit sneezed some blood and watched the demigods begin recreating their formation.

Cheg-Cheg bounded a step forward and landed one-footed on half a dozen of Lutigan's shield-men. Fingit gaped as the monster hopped to the side and squished three more demigods, and then landed with both feet on the remaining unfortunate pawns. Without breaking rhythm, the Void-beast jumped back to his original position to complete the combination.

"That was rather graceful." Sakaj sneered from her knees. "You should ask Cheg-Cheg to dance. I find most mystical creatures to be quite agile. Even the imps."

Fingit wiped his face. "Let's serve tea and read poetry too. If you can read poetry with your lungs hanging out your nose."

Sakaj shrieked a spine-withering battle cry and ran toward Cheg-Cheg. Fingit followed her. He didn't know what had happened to Krak.

Everyone was charging toward the monster, but Casserak was the first to close with it. She lifted her spear with both brown armored arms and jammed it into the earth. The ground jerked and clashed in an expanding earthquake directed toward Cheg-Cheg. Old trees heaved over and fell as the quake passed. It flowed up to the Void-beast and shattered the ground under him. Their enemy flexed his knees and stuck out his arms for balance. The earthquake passed without bobbling the creature.

Cheg-Cheg took a casual step forward before bending and shoveling an enormous pit out of the ground with one swipe of his clawed hand. At the same time, he seized Casserak in his other hand and lifted her. Her spear spun away into the trees. The Void-beast hurled Casserak into the pit hard enough for her brown armor to ring like a dropped pot lid. Then he shoved the dirt back into the pit on top of her and stomped it flat, three times.

Now Harik, his wife Trutch, and the Forest Goddess Chira closed in from three sides, with Harik throwing javelins and Chira shooting arrows up Cheg-Cheg's nose. The monster bent and grabbed Chira by the head and torso. He stood, lifted her, and dropped her into his maw like a sardine. Fingit heard the shriek of monster teeth on the green metal armor, along with the shriek of Chira as she was crushed and consumed. The armor wasn't working out as well as he'd hoped.

Effla and Gorlana were tearing their way through underbrush to join the attack. Fingit and Sakaj were half a minute away. Krak and Lutigan were nowhere in sight. The great monster feinted toward Trutch with his left hand and then snatched Harik with his right. Harik tried to stab the beast in the thumb with his lightning-javelin, but he electrocuted himself. Cheg-Cheg kicked Trutch, and she sailed halfway up the mountainside, a saffron missile. She slammed into the granite slope and sounded like a gong announcing the end of time. Her limp body slid down the slope.

Madimal had retrieved Casserak's spear to charge the monster, with Gorlana screaming profanities at his side. Cheg-Cheg plucked Madimal up with his left hand. Since a squirming Harik filled his other hand, the monster dropped and smashed Gorlana under his horrific knee. He ground Gorlana into the earth as if she were a smoldering ember. When the beast rose, Gorlana did not emerge from the huge divot in which he had smashed her. Her dismembered, sparkly-blue leg *did* emerge, stuck to the monster's knee. Cheg-Cheg shook his leg for a couple of seconds, and the dislodged limb fell to the mangled earth.

Cheg-Cheg stood, lifted Harik and Madimal to his face, and shook them like a child might shake two bugs. Fingit could see Harik's arms flailing and Madimal's feet kicking, but they'd be elevated in moments, on their way to the Dim Lands, and therefore out of the fight. He despised the idea of failing and having to try again tomorrow, and each day after that, over and over, until Cheg-Cheg was injured badly enough—or got bored enough—to leave them alone. Today didn't look like the Day of Victory for the gods, though.

The air crackled above Fingit's head, and every droplet of airborne water boiled away in an instant. The impossibly searing light of the sun streamed out from the mountainside, passed just between Trutch and Harik, and sizzled into Cheg-Cheg's left eyeball. The monster bellowed. It assuredly did not roar. It closed its eyes and shuffled back a step, but it didn't drop the two trapped gods.

The horrific ray of annihilation ceased. Fingit watched Cheg-Cheg's eyelid, expecting to see awful damage, even a hole burned all the way to the monster's brain. But when the eyelid opened, it revealed an intact eyeball, although it was smoking and a little discolored in one spot.

"Damn it!" Krak closed with Fingit and Sakaj as they sprinted. "I may not have killed it, but it knows I don't like it very much."

Now Cheg-Cheg sidestepped away from the remaining gods, produced a titanic grunt, and inscribed an arc on the ground with the longest talon of his right foot, ripping up trees and dislodging boulders as he went. A circle of earth seemed to dissolve within that arc. The monster stepped into the circle and began sinking into the ground, still holding Madimal and Harik.

Despite possessing divine speed and endurance, Fingit wasn't sure he could reach the monster before he disappeared. He also wasn't sure he'd be able to strike much of a blow when he got there. Perhaps it was just as well that Cheg-Cheg's piglike, tufted ears had dropped below ground level when Fingit, Sakaj, Krak, and Effla reached the circle.

Looking down, Fingit saw the monster carrying Harik and Trutch, descending toward a landscape he recognized as Unicorn Town. *They're dead. Cheg-Cheg can destroy them for all time there. What idiot can I trick into going after them?*

"We have to save them!" Fingit yelled. "Let's jump in after them! All together... one... two... three!"

No idiots jumped into the hole. Effla at least had the courtesy to act a little embarrassed. Fingit put the doomed gods out of his thoughts and began considering how to improve the armor's survivability.

A screaming Lutigan hurtled past them, almost knocking Fingit into the hole. Lutigan threw himself into the emptiness, swords upraised, angling for the top of Cheg-Cheg's feather-crested skull. A moment later, the circle solidified back into the regular ground of the forested foothills.

All four gods stared at the spot into which Lutigan had

leaped. Effla shuffled her feet a bit. Sakaj wound and unwound her strangling cord.

"Well, now I feel bad," Fingit said, and the other gods nodded.

Actually, I don't feel bad. I feel... useless. I didn't do a damned thing. I didn't even have to fool Lutigan into doing something stupid. He's just stupid. Aw, no wonder they laugh at me and call me the Little Tinker of the Gods. I'm more like the Limp Dandelion of the Gods.

Fingit grabbed Krak's arm. "Elevate me! Send me to Unicorn Town!"

Krak shook his head. Effla, the Goddess of Love, said, "The monster will kill you there, little boy, and you will be dead ever after. You've never been capable of rising to a challenge."

Fingit blushed but said, "I can stop—" He ceased talking when Sakaj jammed a knife through his throat and dragged it to the side, slicing his jugular. Blood sprayed against his armor's collar and into his eyes, blinding him.

"You cretin!" Krak yelled at Sakaj. "He'll be asleep when he gets there! Helpless!"

Fingit ignored Krak. He clutched his hammer, and as his body collapsed, he focused on Unicorn Town.

SEVENTEEN

(Sakaj)

S akaj wiped Fingit's blood off her face using the back of her hand. "Well?" she said, looking from Krak to Effla and back.

"If you try to stab me, I'll cut you in two from your ratty hair down to your other ratty hair," Effla said.

Sakaj lowered her knife. "We have to go after them."

"No!" Effla said.

"Yes," Krak said at the same time.

Effla took a step back and squinted.

Sakaj stood tall and spoke to Effla as if she were a dim pony. "Cheg-Cheg can take any of us to the Dark Lands whenever he wants and finish us there."

Krak rubbed his jaw. "Either we defeat him today, or we accept exile. Hell, for all we know, he might follow us into the Void and destroy us there."

Effla cursed for a few moments and then nodded. She drew her knife and placed the point on Sakaj's throat. Krak pulled forth his knife, which was quite a lot nicer than any other knife in existence, and laid it against Effla's throat. Sakaj lifted her knife and prepared to slay the Father of the Gods.

Krak cleared his throat. "And... now!"

All three knives were driven forward with divine power, and all three accomplished deicide. Sakaj grinned and held the Dark Lands in mind as she expired.

An unknown interval later, Sakaj awoke lying on velvety black grass. She rolled to her feet and began unwinding the strangling cord from about her forearm. Krak was already sprinting down the shallow hill toward Cheg-Cheg and the not-so-mystical pond. The monster was snapping and grunting a few hundred paces away. Sakaj followed Krak, and she heard Effla's footsteps slapping the grass behind her.

Cheg-Cheg still grasped Harik and Madimal, who remained alive, if flailing and shouting meant anything. Fingit was bouncing and dodging around the monster's left foot, which jerked, stomped, and denied Fingit a good target. Sakaj didn't see Lutigan anywhere.

As the newly arrived gods drew near their enemy, Cheg-Cheg sidestepped and whacked himself on the side of the head twice using the hand still grasping Madimal. Then he wriggled like a horse's back in fly season. Madimal screamed and began babbling. He babbled so loudly that Sakaj almost didn't hear Lutigan yelling and hooting from above. After a moment of disorientation, she realized that Lutigan was inside Cheg-Cheg's ear, probably scrambling around in the ear canal and whacking everything within reach.

Cheg-Cheg must have tired of Madimal's terrified gibberish, because he squeezed his fist tight and crushed the god, armor and all. Madimal jabbered, then burbled, then whimpered, and then he was silent, except for the plop of some entrails and one arm as they fell to the grass. The beast pitched his corpse, which spun away over the pond, the trees, and whatever lay beyond them.

Cheg-Cheg slapped his ear with his open hand, but Lutigan never stopped yelling defiance and profanity. Krak released the impossibly searing light of the sun at the monster's undamaged eye, but Cheg-Cheg warded the light-beam away with his other hand, almost annihilating Harik.

The beast snarled and then spit at Krak, Sakaj, and Effla. Krak jumped one way, Sakaj jumped the other, and Effla stumbled for an instant. A great, viscous mass of Cheg-Cheg's acid-like spittle enveloped her and smashed her to the ground. Sakaj bounced back to her and noted that the corrosive substance hadn't marred Fingit's armor, or at least not yet.

Cheg-Cheg had paused for a moment while aiming his sputum. Fingit now charged toward the monster's stupendous right foot and swung his hammer with both hands. He landed the blow against the foot's longest talon, and a shattering boom caused Sakaj to squint and hold her ears. When she opened her eyes again, she saw that the talon had been smashed completely off and was lying atop Fingit, who'd been thrown to the ground. Cheg-Cheg cocked his head at the god, who was struggling to stand. The monster shifted his weight and stomped Fingit with a cataclysmic reverberation.

Sakaj rushed past Krak toward the creature. Krak released the impossibly searing light of the sun again, this time striking Cheg-Cheg in the mouth. The Void-beast shook his head and leaned to step away, but he halted halfway through the motion. He looked down and wiggled his talons, and then the creature tried to lift the foot that had crushed Fingit. The foot was bound fast to the earth. Cheg-Cheg dropped Harik, who plunged two hundred feet into the nearby pond, howling all the way. The monster grabbed his black leathery lower leg with both of his clawed hands. He heaved on the leg, which stretched like cooling taffy, soft and pliable.

"Hold this!" Sakaj yelled, throwing one end of her strangling cord to Krak. She sprinted between Cheg-Cheg's feet at supernatural speed, holding the other end of the cord, which lengthened as she ran. She rounded the monster's immobilized heel and returned to Krak. Then she and Krak crossed the cord and pulled it tight around Cheg-Cheg's ankle.

Cheg-Cheg swatted at the gods, but with one foot pinned and a god ravaging his inner ear, he bobbled and even staggered once. Krak and Sakaj heaved in opposite directions with every grain of their divine strength, as if they were using an enchanted wire to slice an enormous, mystical Void-cheese. Fingit had made the strangling cord long and strong. The cord closed, the ankle severed with a gigantic, wet pop, and the monster dropped to his knees in a catastrophic collapse.

Krak and Sakaj ran back out of Cheg-Cheg's reach. The beast just watched them run away, crouched on his hands and knees. He gazed at them with his feathery brow drawn tight and his lips turned down over a mouthful of decimating teeth.

Sakaj regarded the Void-beast. *This is the worst we've ever hurt him. Perhaps he's accusing us of cheating at some rough but collegial game. Perhaps he's going to cry. He could sing and break wind in harmony for all I care, as long as he goes away.*

The monster poked at his dismembered right foot and then jiggled it. The foot appeared to no longer be locked tight to the earth. Cheg-Cheg picked up the foot, examined it, and then looked around before stuffing the appendage between his teeth. Lutigan jumped out of the monster's ear and dropped to the earth, where he landed with simian grace.

Cheg-Cheg, Dark Annihilator of the Void and Vicinity, crawled away on his hands and knees, carrying his foot in his mouth. Just as he disappeared into the Unicorn Town darkness, Sakaj shouted, "Don't come back! Your foot's not the only thing we can cut off!"

Sakaj and Krak trotted to the deep depression that Cheg-Cheg's severed foot had left behind. They found Fingit lying in the bottom, dazed and squeaking, but alive in his unscratched armor. They hauled him upright and steadied him as he climbed out of the depression, stumbling and drooling.

When Fingit had been revived somewhat, he said, "I figured I'd get stomped on. I mean, if you hit a giant monster on the foot with a hammer, expect to get stomped on, right? So I planned for that contingency. A bit tougher armor, a few special enchantments blended to be extra-sticky and extra-stretchy, and there you go."

"Risky. Too damned risky, and not much of a plan," Krak said.

"Maybe," Sakaj said. "But it worked." She spotted Lutigan dragging a half-drowned but still-wiggling Harik to shore.

Fingit let his head fall back, and he shrugged. "If all this happened like I planned, I figured you'd know what to do. If it didn't, then I'd be dead and wouldn't give a crap anyway."

Sakaj smiled and kissed Fingit on the cheek, then she patted him on his armored head. "Sneaky bastard."

EIGHTEEN

(Fingit)

No one had peed on Fingit all morning, which made him feel a little victorious. He rolled onto his back on the luscious grass that smelled sweet enough to eat. The sun dusted warmth onto his face, and the breeze brushed it away.

A paw like iron drove into his diaphragm, and another slapped his upper thigh. He gushed air, and a tongue of unparalleled determination tried to lick the inside of his mouth. At least the dog had learned not to pee on him. Laughing, Fingit pushed away the tongue and the furry head it belonged in. "No! Bad dog." The dog backed away a step and barked as Fingit sat up. As soon as the god was steady, the dog bounded onto him and began licking his ear. Fingit hugged the solid, shaggy, unexceptional beast around the neck, and the creature sat on his foot.

Fingit had put some thought into making this dog, and he wanted it sufficiently prepared for its purpose. He reached behind him and flung a large stick he'd brought. He reminded himself to hold back. Now that Fingit possessed his godlike physique once again, he could toss the stick past the estate walls with no effort.

The dog galloped away and returned with the stick by the time Fingit had stood. It offered Fingit the stick, which he grasped. Then the dog refused to give it up, tugging and shaking its head.

Pretty good so far.

Later that morning, after Fingit and the dog had enjoyed a modest interval of jumping, barking, and drooling, Sakaj walked onto Fingit's estate. Her rapid, sinuous, and disdainful stride brought her through the platinum gates set into immense, green marble columns. Upon seeing Fingit with the dog, she halted. "You needn't limit your acquaintances to your intellectual equals. I'll use short words when I talk to you from now on."

Fingit hid his annoyance by chuckling and scratching the dog's loose neck skin. Sakaj had become increasingly sharp and even cruel to him in the days since they'd maimed and vanquished Cheg-Cheg. She had accused him of trying to steal her glory just because he'd banged out a few trinkets and gotten crushed. Fingit had explained that glory was flying around in abundance these days, and he didn't need any of hers. She had clarified that all the glory was hers. He didn't want to go to war against Sakaj, especially when he'd just rebuilt all his dwellings, but she was acting crazy even for her.

"Come on, Krak's waiting," Sakaj said. "You can bring your mistress."

"Krak can wait. This fine beast is yours. It's a present." He clapped the dog's shoulder and stepped back.

Sakaj rolled her eyes and walked away toward the gate. "I'm going. I didn't want to bring you, anyway. I'll tell Krak you're off plotting to murder him. Since you're so glorious now."

"Wait, you'll want this dog. It's special."

"I heard about the dog you made for Krak. No thanks."

"Just wait!" Fingit yelled.

Sakaj turned, cocked one hip, and lifted her jaw at him.

Fingit pointed at the animal, which sat and began scratching its ear. "Even though you're an aggravating, prevaricating, deranged, treacherous serpent and you'd melt me in lava if it suited you, I feel like being nice. You need this dog."

Sakaj crossed her arms. "Oh, of course I do. You must think I need something to love. That will make me gentle and floppy like you, correct?"

"Not at all." Fingit gave her an innocent look.

Sakaj sneered. "All right, you must think I'm stupid enough to take a dog that's booby-trapped or cursed."

"No. I think you need something to kick that will still love you."

Sakaj frowned at Fingit. Then she looked at the dog, which was now licking its rectum. "Well... that wouldn't be any fun. No challenge."

"You never know. Maybe you'll feel lazy some afternoon. Regarding booby traps, I'll disassemble her down to the screws and gears so you can inspect her."

"Never mind that. I can see that you're telling the truth. You're so transparent. And gullible. I used you like an old rag."

"You certainly did."

"Did you name the creature? Probably something pedestrian such as Floppy or Scraps."

"Not exactly." Fingit cleared his throat. "I inscribed a hundred lead balls with a different letter on each, put them in a sack, and drew out seven without looking at them. I laid them in a row on the anvil, still not looking, and then I threw them into the forge. No one ever saw what they spelled, so the dog's name is, well, unknowable."

Sakaj looked away, but not before Fingit saw her grin. She said, "Does it do any tricks?"

"Only one. Say the name of the being you hate most in all existence."

Looking back at Fingit and the dog, Sakaj whispered, "Harik."

Three dozen six-foot-long spikes sprang out of the dog in all directions. It resembled a panting, flop-eared, twelve-foot-diameter hedgehog with spines like needle-tipped razors.

Sakaj raised her eyebrows at Fingit.

"It only works when you say it. Say anything else."

"Uh..."

The spikes retracted into the dog with a well-machined click. The dog ran to Sakaj with worshipful eyes, and it sniffed her crotch.

Sakaj guided the dog's nose elsewhere and gave it a couple of hesitant pats on the head. "Let's go then. Krak's waiting to laud me." She and the dog strode away toward the gate.

"You're welcome," Fingit said as he followed her.

The Gossamer Forest stretched out full and verdant under the midday sun. That sun hadn't returned to golden, not even close. But it showered wholesome yellow light onto the Home of the Gods. Forest creatures darted around, no longer foul and warped, except for the squirrels. To Fingit they still appeared foul and warped, but he'd thought squirrels looked that way since squirrels first existed.

Fingit and Sakaj descended into a shallow, emerald glen of heartbreaking serenity. A modest pond lay at its center, as pure and poignant as a tear. Artful foliage dotted the pond's grass-napped banks. Benches, tables, and divans of marble and rare woods had been placed around the pond in architectural tension. The breeze channeled wafts of lilac and rosemary, brushing the water and caressing the branches of the lone tree in the glen, a noble golden cypress. As Fingit strolled down into this newly created sanctuary, he felt that it might be the most peaceful place in all existence.

"Welcome to the Vale of Righteous Devastation!" Krak bellowed as they reached the pond to stand with the rest of the gods. "We have pierced the Veil. We have freed ourselves. We have reached once more into the world of man." Krak waved at the pond. "We have wrought this, the Theater of Man, into which we may see to guide and protect man once again."

Fingit gazed at the pond's surface. He applied a slight thought about the Nub, and an image appeared, shifting toward the boy but leaving the rest of the pond undisturbed. Now all of the gods could visit the world of man as they wished. He shook himself and looked back at Krak, hoping he hadn't been caught letting his attention wander.

I'd hate to have the impossibly searing light of the sun shot up my nose for being an inattentive little squid.

Krak was still speaking. "We owe our survival as divine beings, and our deliverance from the greatest peril of all time, to that which I am ashamed to say we have least understood and least appreciated throughout the eons."

Sakaj took a deep breath.

"Our rightful power and majesty were delivered to us by our will to work together, to toss away our grudges and hurts, and to entrust our lives—our true and eternal lives—to one another."

Sakaj didn't move, but Fingit heard the breath being pressed out of her as if she were a frog stepped on by a bull. He glanced around and saw that Harik was scowling at the grass, and Lutigan looked like he'd swallowed a dead skunk.

Krak went on: "It is my wish that we set aside pettiness so that we may become inviolable and indestructible for all time."

"What about me?" Sakaj said.

"Eh?"

"What about me? I elevated myself hundreds of times to find the Dark Lands, I brought Fingit there to work for us, and I secured the power that brought us victory, which required me to make an awful deal, by the way. And what about Cheg-Cheg's foot?"

Krak looked down and smiled. "Well, I didn't want to mention it, but I suppose I did contribute more than most. I provided the fundamental strength required to dismember the Void-beast."

Sakaj took a step forward and said, "What? I brought us victory. The glory is mine. I should get a tithe on all power passing through these lands."

Krak laughed. "That's entertaining! Only I get a portion of all trades. It's always been that way. I'm... the Father of the Gods. I agree that you contributed like a regular warrior, Sakaj. You served us well. Oh, and Fingit helped too."

Fingit touched Sakaj's arm, but she flung off his hand. "I will see this land in flaming wreckage before I let this stand!"

Krak stopped smiling and seemed to grow half again as tall. "This is a time to rejoice. It's a celebration of our collective victory and our resplendent future." He rubbed his hands together, and slivers of shocking-white light leaked out from his palms. "I would hate to tarnish the mood by burning off someone's tender parts."

Sakaj trembled, and Fingit stepped away so that his tender parts didn't get vaporized in error. Then she exhaled, looked down, and stepped back.

"Good!" Krak said. "I think everything's been said, so let us revel! Bring the ambrosia!"

Demigods and demigoddesses hurried into the glen bearing pitchers, platters, bowls, and pipes. Fingit didn't partake much, but not because he felt cheated. He didn't really want glory, anyway. He wanted a well-stocked workshop, plenty of power, and everyone else to leave him alone until he needed guinea pigs. In fact, he had a new idea. He'd given up on chariots, but perhaps a flying war elephant powered by the impossibly searing light of the sun... he'd need to make some calculations.

The party wallowed its way deep into the evening darkness, with every indication it would continue for several days. Fingit shuffled away while Weldt was telling a joke about four water spirits and a sea serpent. Halfway to the Gossamer Forest, he heard the dog barking behind him, so he stopped and waited for Sakaj to catch up.

Her hair, black as night and soft as sleep, trapped specks of moonlight so that her head appeared to be covered in stars. Her face was shadowed and still. She stood straight and relaxed. She didn't speak, but she did scratch the dog's ear.

At last, Fingit said, "Well, that was a kick-in-the-groin, huh?"

Sakaj nodded.

"I guess you've got a lot of work to do, since you owe the Nub power every day."

She nodded again.

"Whatever it is you want, I'm not helping you. Take your dog and go home."

"Thank you for my dog." Fingit heard the smile in her voice. "She's beautiful."

"Stop that. Don't be nice. It doesn't suit you."

Sakaj knelt and put her arms around the dog's neck. The animal panted, wagged its tail, and wiggled in happiness. "You know, we're the only two beings in existence who have ever elevated Krak. You've elevated him more than once."

Fingit halted with a stomp. "No! No talk about elevating Krak! I'll remind you that he now knows how to destroy insolent gods forever."

"I'm not saying we should really kill him permanently! It's just... interesting that it can be done. Of course, you were only able to elevate old, degenerate, insane Krak. Elevating mighty Krak is probably impossible. Killing him must be impossible beyond doubt."

"Well... probably. I guess nothing's totally impossible. But shut up about it!"

"Right! Silly of me. Just as an intellectual exercise, what would it take?"

Fingit laughed. "You can't stop, can you? Do you think I'm stupid? You can't use me anymore."

Sakaj stood and sighed. "I guess you're right. You must already have lots of fascinating problems to solve. I'm sorry. I'll fetch you a drink to apologize."

"Fine. Just one. A small one."

Sakaj took Fingit's hand in one of hers, and she petted her dog with the other. Then she led them both through the trees toward the Sun Soul Pavilion.

Fingit chuckled. *I can't believe she'd try to fool me again. She must think I'm an idiot. She's the one who's transparent now. I'm glad she likes the dog, though.*

Damn, it is an interesting problem. What would it take to really kill Krak?

HAVE YOU READ DEATH'S COLLECTOR?

Cursed to take lives for the God of Death. Sorcerers must give up things and people they love, or accept things they despise, to gain magical power. The sorcerer Bib saves his daughter by accepting a curse to murder people, and only Death knows how many Bib must kill. He tries to slay only evil people, but soon finds he's also killing people who are merely bad, or who might someday become bad. Bib chases a brutal sorcerer to help a woman rescue her boy, mainly because he expects a lot of killing. But he doesn't expect to unearth obscure magic, enslave spiteful supernatural beings, and strike ghastly bargains with the childish gods. And the last thing he expects is to face the question—is he a good man cursed to crave murder, or has he always been a murderer at heart?

Read the Death-Cursed Wizard Book 1 now:
https://tinyurl.com/y36t2ryt

ABOUT THE AUTHOR

BILL MCCURRY holds a Bachelor of Arts in Sociology and a Master of Arts in Sociology from the University of Texas at Arlington. He is one of seven people known to have secured a non-academic job using a sociology degree. Bill's short story "The Santa Fix" was published by Open Heart Publishing's anthology *An Honest Lie: Volume 3*. He has performed and taught improv and interactive theater for over twenty years. During his career, Bill has owned a small construction company, run market research projects, managed customer service groups, and developed computer systems as a contractor for the National Cancer Institute. He is currently writing his seventh novel, *Death's Least Favorite Toy*. Bill grew up in Fort Worth, Texas, and now lives in Carrollton, Texas, with his wife, Kathleen, an independent court reporter who is so keenly determined that she would always be able to kill him if it came to a knife fight.

CONNECT WITH THE AUTHOR
BILL-MCCURRY.COM
TWITTER.COM/BILLMCCURRY
GOODREADS.COM/AUTHOR/SHOW/5427659
FACEBOOK: HTTPS://WWW.FACEBOOK.COM/BILL.MCCURRY3/
AMAZON.COM/BILL-MCCURRY/E/B0068PO2AA

Made in the USA
Coppell, TX
13 December 2020

44568952R00104